EVOLUTION

EVOLUTION

THE GHOST SQUADRON BOOK 3

SARAH NOFFKE
MICHAEL ANDERLE

DISRUPTIVE IMAGINATION

EVOLUTION TEAM

For Lydia. My greatest treasure in the universe.
-Sarah

To Family, Friends and
Those Who Love
To Read.
May We All Enjoy Grace
To Live the Life We Are
Called.
- Michael

Defiance Trading Company Headquarters, Planet L2SCQ-6 in Frontier space.

Felix Castile listened to the loud breathing of the Kezzin behind him. Commander Lytes had to have a deviated septum. It was the only plausible reason for his constant sniffling, which was always interrupting the silence.

Or maybe it was just a physical trait of the Kezzin. Felix hadn't taken much time to learn about the species. He knew these lizard-type aliens could stop breathing for an extended period, but that was about it.

Felix prided himself on his ability to accumulate and use information, but only when it was useful. If it didn't earn him additional power or prestige, he didn't seek the data out. His current relationship with Commander Lytes existed solely to further his plan, which was the complete and absolute destruction of General Lance Reynolds. The moment the Kezzin stopped being useful was the moment Felix would cut him loose.

All that Felix Castile did was for the goal. Every action, every day.

And that was exactly why he was here in this awful place, staring at a group of black market merchants.

The leader of the Defiance Trading Company, a rogue operation that stockpiled weapons and sold them on the black market, looked up from the pad in his hand. "We have loaded everything that you requested into your ship, but I have yet to see the funds come over though," said the man. His voice was raspy, probably from years of smoking or hanging out in filthy warehouses like this one. The trader, Mateo, had a thick scar that ran over his left eye and down his cheek. Living outside of Federation space hadn't been kind to him—that much was clear.

Felix surveyed Mateo's crew. There were roughly a dozen men stationed around the warehouse, most of them with their guns at the ready and grimaces on their greasy faces. Felix was flanked by Brotherhood soldiers, but they were outnumbered by Mateo's guards. No doubt the arms dealer felt safe with all these people to protect him.

He was wrong, though. Only fools underestimated Felix, and the arms merchant would soon understand that.

Felix cleared his throat. "You sold me three nukes. How many more do you have here?"

Mateo's scar moved when he lifted his eyebrow. "Not sure why my inventory is any business of yours. I supplied you with what you asked for."

"That you did," Felix said, pulling his hat down over his eyes and taking a step backward.

Mateo eyed the pad again. "Like I mentioned, the transfer hasn't come through. We can't let you leave until it does. It's simple business—I'm sure you understand."

Felix smiled darkly. "About that…"

He took a few more steps back, and his soldiers stepped in to shield him.

"Didn't you hear me?" asked Mateo. "Hey, I'm talking to—"

Shots were fired from above, and Mateo's men yelled. Some tried to return fire, but they were quickly silenced.

Felix turned in time to watch Mateo clutch his chest as the bullet pierced the arms dealer's flesh. Disbelief and betrayal rang out in the man's eyes as he fell to his knees, then collapsed forward.

Each of the men stationed around the warehouse lay in similar positions, blood puddling around them. None had stood a chance.

Stationed overhead were a dozen Brotherhood soldiers, each assigned to take out a specified target on the ground. Their timing had been perfect.

Felix glanced up to the rafters with a proud look in his eyes. "Have your people load the remaining weapons into my ship."

"Yes, sir," said Commander Lytes, his eyes lingering on one of the dead bodies for a moment. He hadn't liked the plan and said there had to be another way, but Lytes had been wrong—surely he had seen that by now. Perhaps next time he would trust Felix's plans from the beginning.

The exit door swung open in front of them, and a man with a short black Mohawk and a leather jacket that had seen better days froze on the threshold. He scanned the warehouse, his eyes falling first on Mateo's dead body and then the others that were strewn all over the facility. His gaze snapped to Felix, who was standing roughly ten meters away.

They'd missed one of Mateo's men. "Get him!" barked Felix.

The soldiers darted forward, right as the strange man reversed, heading back the way he came. Gun shots rang out from the hallway, echoing loudly in the warehouse.

Felix looked at Commander Lytes. "Have your soldiers search the building. I don't want anyone left alive, do you understand? No witnesses."

Commander Lytes nodded and hurried off to where his people were gathering in the middle of the facility after climbing down from the rafters in which they had been stationed.

Felix's eyes briefly rested on Mateo's dead body. Perhaps he would have been happy to know that his weapons would be used to end a long-standing feud, in a fight that would shake the very foundations of the galaxy. What better use could a man like Mateo have than to aid Felix's mission? What better purpose could there be than to alter the status quo? Had Mateo not come to this warehouse today, he might never have realized his true destiny. He would have gone on living his life, worthless as it was, and died without ever truly mattering.

But Felix would make him matter. Felix would give Mateo's life purpose. That would be his gift to him, albeit a posthumous one.

Soon everything would be in place to make General

Reynolds pay. Felix had figured out the best way to punish him for what he'd done all those years ago.

Break the Federation, and General Reynolds would be broken, too.

As Knox Gunnerson sprinted down the hallway he thought about what he'd seen. They were dead. All of them. That was Mateo's body at the front. They'd killed him. They'd killed all of them.

He could hear soldiers pounding, drawing closer to him. Knox's feet weren't moving fast enough, and the hallway was too long. There was nowhere to hide. What was he going to do?

The noise behind him stopped, but he didn't dare turn around or slow down. Instead, he pushed forward faster. *Only fifteen meters to the exit. He was almost—*

A bullet whizzed by his skull and struck the door ahead. He turned to see two Brotherhood soldiers, each holding a rapid-fire rifle.

Knox ducked as the next round was fired, dropping to the ground and rolling to get out of the way.

He pulled his pistol as he rounded the corner, and then halted and took a steadying breath. Pausing to breathe seemed dumb right now, but missing would be fatal.

He racked the gun's slide and released it to load a round into the chamber, then paused to listen to the footsteps of the soldiers as they continued through the hall. He had to wait until they were close enough. Until the moment was perfect.

Knox fired at the Brotherhood soldier in the lead and the male fell back, the hit to his shoulder knocking him down. Knox let out a breath as he released the trigger and prepared for the next shot.

The other soldier had stopped and raised his gun as he tried to find the target, and again Knox pulled the trigger, letting two successive shots fly. The first bullet missed, but the second went straight through the Kezzin's leg and he fell forward onto his hands and knees.

The male stared up at Knox, a desperate look in his eyes. The soldier behind him, still alive, had crawled over to his gun and managed to grasp it.

Knox whipped around and sprinted for the exit, with both these males disabled there was no reason to stay and fight. He didn't have to kill them, as long as he could get away.

Besides, more soldiers would be here soon. He didn't have long.

He managed to get to his ship and open the hatch. It was an old Black Eagle that had seen better days—*too many* days, actually.

Knox had salvaged this bird a few years back and fixed her up as best he could. Mateo had taught him how to fly back when he had first gotten the old ship working. That skill was going to hopefully save his life now. He dropped into his chair, not even strapping in as he started the engines.

"Gonna be a fast takeoff," he said to himself. The engine stalled briefly, but that was normal. Knox slammed his hand onto the controls. "No, you don't. Don't fuck with me today. This isn't the time."

From the side window he saw multiple Brotherhood soldiers spilling out of the ship they'd arrived on, the vessel known as the *Unsurpassed*. Knox had never seen anything quite like it. Massive and smooth by design, it had more guns and weaponry than any single ship should have.

The soldiers fired at his ship just as the booster kicked in and the Black Eagle rose, shots ricocheting off his craft with a series of *clangs*.

Knox fixed his eyes on the clouds as he rocketed away. "You've taken worse. Hang in there, ol' girl," he told his ship, pulling back on the controls and lifting her nose.

He took several potentially fatal hits before the bird managed to soar into space. If he were lucky, he'd make it out of the system. He already knew those guys would follow him—people like that never left survivors—but if he could get far enough away then maybe they wouldn't find him. Maybe he could stay alive.

There were very few things Knox was actually good at, but one of them was hiding.

He'd been doing it all his life.

2

Officers Lounge, QBS *ArchAngel*, Lorialis System

"You're kidding me," said Eddie, pulling back his arm and launching the dart. It whirred through the air and stuck hard into the board a few centimeters from the bullseye.

Lars replaced Eddie at the line. "I'm *not* kidding you! Marilla says these aliens are telepathic. Isn't that bizarre?" He threw his own dart, and it pierced one of the numbers that bordered the target.

"I definitely don't want to meet any of those guys," remarked Eddie. "I don't need some alien in my thoughts." He picked up another dart and twirled it in his fingers. The idea of having someone in his head—like Julianna had Pip —was a bit strange. Sure, there were the obvious perks to it depending on the circumstances, but Eddie wasn't sure how he'd feel about an AI listening to the things that went on in his mind let alone an alien.

Maybe that was why Julianna had gotten rid of her last

AI, Ricky Bobby. Eddie had been silently investigating the whole thing for a while now, ever since Pip had become sentient. Julianna acted happy about the evolution, but there was something else going on. He could sense it in little ways. It wasn't so much what she said, but what she didn't say. When Eddie had discovered Ricky Bobby's existence, it had come as a shock. He knew her well now, but Julianna had never spoken about her former AI companion, despite how long she and Ricky Bobby had worked together.

Eddie wanted to approach her about this, but had yet to do so. He wasn't sure why. Maybe he just didn't know if it was his place.

"Yeah, I know," said Lars. "One or two telepaths is one thing, but an entire species boggles my mind." The Kezzin soldier watched as Eddie took his second shot and again narrowly missed the bullseye.

Lars didn't bother lining up for his next shot, just threw the dart haphazardly. It didn't even make it to the board.

Eddie whistled through his teeth. "Damn! I'm glad you fly better than you shoot, or you'd have been wasted by now."

Lars shook his head. He realized he was being sloppy. It had been like this in recent weeks during his down time. That was the only opportunity he had to let his mind wander, and it always shot back to the Brotherhood. The idea of the army Commander Lytes had put together overwhelmed Lars whenever he thought about it, but he couldn't help but dwell on it. Maybe he didn't know those soldiers, but they were still fellow Kezzin. They were his brothers.

He wondered about his family too. Had his brother been required to join once Lars had left? He didn't like to think about that, but it was difficult to control where his mind went. Doubts and fears were tricky things to control —the moment you thought you had a handle on them, they consumed you.

The screen on an adjacent wall flickered on and Chester's pale face peered at Eddie and Lars. "There you are, Captain," he said, beaming. "There's something I think you should take a look at."

Eddie, unflustered, pulled back his arm and released his third dart, which went straight into the bullseye this time. Casually, as though he had planned it, he turned to the monitor. "I'll be right over. Have you paged Commander Fregin yet?"

"Yes, she's on her way," said Chester, running his hands through his spiky blond hair.

"Very well." Eddie slapped Lars on the shoulder as he turned to leave. "Keep practicing, brother. One of these days you'll be able to beat me."

Lars smirked, showing his razor-sharp teeth. "Challenge accepted."

Intelligence Center, QBS *ArchAngel*, Lorialis System

Julianna was already in the Intelligence Center when Eddie arrived.

Harley ran over and wagged his tail at him, tongue hanging limply from his mouth. Eddie knelt and tousled the dog's head.

"Hey there, Jules. Saw the list of new recruits you brought in. We're starting to fill out a bit, aren't we?" Eddie smiled at Marilla, who was hunched over her desk as usual.

"Not as fast as I'd like, but we're making progress," said Julianna. She gave Chester a nod to let him know to proceed with the briefing.

Chester smiled. "Thanks for coming so fast. I only just picked up on this, but I thought you both might want to see it," he said, blowing up the image on the largest screen above his desk. "This shot was taken from Federation Border Station 7."

He zoomed in on the image until a small ship came into view, and Eddie raised his brow. It was a Black Eagle, albeit heavily modified. It seemed to be painted light gray, unlike the standard charcoal color Eddie was used to seeing. There were black streaks on the nose that looked almost like whiskers, and something on the side that resembled a fin.

"What's going on?" asked Eddie, stepping forward and narrowing his eyes. "What's a Black Eagle doing out there, and why does it look like someone pulled it apart and pieced it back together? Don't tell me that's a Federation ship!"

"I don't think so," said Chester, "which was one of the reasons I alerted you. This guy, from everything I've been able to tell, just flew in from the Frontier. I don't think he realized he was close enough to Station 7 for anyone to get a shot of him."

"How did you get this feed?" asked Julianna.

"I picked up some of the comm traffic from Station 7. They sent a message when he was close enough, but he cut the line as soon as it happened. He tried his best to stay off the radar."

"Tried?" asked Eddie.

"Well, he *did* sever the line with Station 7, but I had already leeched into his comm, which granted me the opportunity to track his movements." Chester rubbed his hands together with a cunning look in his eyes.

"You're one smart sonofabitch. Have I told you lately I'm glad you're on our side?" said Eddie with a laugh.

"You haven't said it nearly often enough for my liking," joked Chester.

"He enjoys having his ego stroked more than Harley likes his head scratched," said Marilla, not looking away from her screen.

"It's true, I'm just like a dog." Chester tapped on his keyboard, enlarging the image of the ship even more. "Anyway, just before the comm was severed completely I heard the guy in this rogue ship say, 'Damn Federation can't protect me from the Brotherhood. No one can.'"

"Brotherhood? He said that?" Julianna asked, standing up straighter. Harley had been eyeing her eagerly, as if hoping she'd acknowledge him or maybe even pet him, but she'd kept her eyes trained on the image over Chester's desk.

"Yeah, that was what got my attention and is why you're here," said Chester.

"What's that on the side of the ship?" asked Eddie.

"I've been trying to find out. The image is getting cleaned, so I'm hoping a clearer version refreshes soon. The cameras on Station 7 aren't the greatest, so we should be grateful they captured what they did." Chester pushed up his glasses just as the image refreshed, the magnified text on the side of the Black Eagle now readable.

"'DTC?'" asked Julianna, squinting. "Am I reading this right?"

"I've seen that before," said Eddie. "Not long ago, when I was visiting a fringe planet."

"You mean when you were taking a drunken tour of bars on shitty planets?" asked Julianna.

"Yes, actually," said Eddie, winking. "Tons of bar fights, lots of waking up in alleys. Good times."

"What's it stand for?" asked Marilla, poking her head above her desk.

Eddie thought for a moment. "Defiance Trading Company, if I remember right," he finally answered. "They deal in black market weapons. I heard the Federation pushed them beyond their borders a long time ago. I don't know much more than that about them, though."

"Which means, if this guy is flying around next to the border—" began Julianna.

"Then something's gone wrong," Eddie said, completing her sentence as his gaze drew distant.

"Something involving the Brotherhood, it sounds like," said Julianna.

"Yeah. If they're after him, there has to be a reason. I'm guessing this guy could tell us some stories." Eddie stood tall, the adrenaline already starting to pound in his veins. "Commander," he said, glancing at Julianna, "you up for an impromptu game of hide and seek?"

She grinned. "Absolutely."

Marilla chimed in with, "I'm guessing this guy is going to do his best to give you the slip. He sounds scared."

Eddie nodded. "Which means we need to double our odds, so I'll have Lars come along. We can practice that pincer movement we were talking about yesterday," said Eddie, his voice growing more excited.

Julianna smirked. "Thanks, Chester, for keeping your eyes on the radar and constantly scanning. Good work."

Chester leaned back and laced his hands behind his head. "Someone has to have eyes out there."

3

Alpha-line Q-Ship, Federation Border Station 7 Airspace, Lorialis System

"That's the Omega-line? It doesn't look any different from *this* Q-Ship," said Lars from the copilot seat.

"That's kind of the point," said Eddie. "The differences are on the inside." He pulled the controls to the side as Julianna maneuvered the other ship, the one Hatch had just created, up next to them. "Strong Arm," he said, using Julianna's call sign, "you wanna show Carnivore what that baby can do?"

"I thought you'd never ask," said Julianna over the comm. The Q-Ship she was flying punched out at breakneck speed, leaving the other behind.

"Whoa, it can definitely *move*," remarked Lars. "I'll admit that's impressive, but I thought the new line had some out-of-this-world features?" The Kezzin gave Eddie a sideways glance that showed his disappointment.

Eddie activated the thrusters to send their own Q-Ship

racing after Julianna. "Just wait. There's another feature you have to see in action."

"Carnivore, did you just say 'out-of-this-world' while we're racing through space?" asked Julianna.

Eddie snickered. "He's been sheltered, so give him a break. We'll teach him some fun references."

A laugh echoed across the comm. "Don't learn your lingo from Blackbeard."

"Hey, I know things!" argued Eddie.

"If you three are done shooting the breeze, our target is ahead," said Pip.

"'Shooting the breeze?'" asked Eddie, activating the second thruster to catch up with Julianna.

"Yes, it's one of the many weird things about his new evolution," said Julianna, a sudden edge to her voice.

Eddie shot Lars a look and raised his eyebrow but said nothing, and Lars returned the glance with a slight shrug.

"Target spotted," said Lars, checking the radar. Julianna, as planned, had made an arc around the upcoming Black Eagle.

"That puppy is slow. It must have been kept in a rusty garage since it was decommissioned." Eddie sent the Q-Ship toward the flying target, doubling his speed.

"Strong Arm, we are approaching and will be in position soon," Lars informed Julianna.

"Fifteen seconds," supplied Pip.

"Almost there," muttered Eddie.

"Target's fuel reserves are low. Engines have failed twice," Pip informed them.

Lars flipped two switches overhead before adjusting his microphone. "Defiance Trading Company, we've determined that your spacecraft is in distress. We're a Ronin tow craft, and we offer assistance."

There was no answer over the static-filled comm, but the gray Black Eagle immediately spun in the opposite direction. For a moment it looked like it would stall, but the engines kicked back on and it shot forward.

"We've got a runner," said Eddie, sitting up.

"Your engines are failing, Defiance. We can help you. We mean you no harm," said Lars over the comm.

Another voice finally answered. "I don't need any help. I've got a rescue craft already on the way."

Eddie sent the Q-Ship after the Black Eagle and quickly caught up. The craft in front of them came to an automatic halt, causing Eddie to swerve the Q-Ship around it. He overshot it by a short distance before doubling back and hovering just in front of the old craft.

"Fuel levels on Defiant ship are nearly depleted," said Pip.

"How long could he idle?" asked Eddie.

"Three hours, roughly," said Pip.

"I don't have three hours to hang around here," remarked Eddie. "This idiot needs to realize we aren't the bad guys."

"Unless he turns out to be an enemy, and then we'll fuck him up," said Julianna.

"There you are, Strong Arm. What say we end this already?" Eddie and Lars were only thirty meters from the other ship, close enough for a visual, and Eddie leaned forward to look into the Black Eagle. The murky dust covering the windows made it impossible to discern a figure, though.

"There's a problem," said Pip over the comm.

"Of course there is. Wouldn't be a party without one," said Eddie, not at all deterred.

"Fuel level is rising," informed the AI

"How is that possible? You said it was near zero," said Lars.

"It *shouldn't* be possible," said Eddie. "Maybe there was a malfunction with the gauge." As soon as the last word left his mouth the rogue Black Eagle zoomed forward again in another attempt to get away. It wasn't going to work, but the last-ditch effort was kind of cute. Eddie flew straight after it and kept pace.

"Have you guys been looking for me?" asked Julianna. Eddie couldn't see her out the window, but a quick glance at the radar told him that she was hovering just above the Black Eagle.

"There you are!" Eddie chuckled. "Lars, tell this guy we've got him surrounded. You've got a nice voice, so I'm sure it'll sound comforting."

Lars shot Eddie a strange look. "'Comforting?' Do I really?"

"Like an old grandmother," Eddie assured him.

"If she had smoked for forty years," added Julianna.

"Are you sure you want me to say we have him surrounded?" asked Lars. "We only have two ships."

Keeping his hands on the controls, Eddie nodded. "Just do it."

Without another word, Lars flipped a switch. "Defiance, we have you surrounded and we mean you no harm. Allow us to tow you from here."

"I'm not falling for your bullshit. Just leave me alone." The voice crackled through the staticky comm.

"Testy little tyke, isn't he?" asked Eddie. "Strong Arm, we're ready for you to graduate to the next phase."

"Copy," said Julianna. "Initiating. Be ready for next phase in three, two...and one."

In front of the racing Black Eagle another Q-Ship appeared, and Lars' eyes widened with shock. Eddie had wanted to tell him about this part beforehand, but he had also wanted it to be a surprise. He wagered there was no danger in that.

Lars whipped his gaze to the radar. Another ship had appeared behind the Black Eagle and almost at once the fleeing ship slowed, stalling once more before coming to a near-halt. A second later two more Q-Ships materialized on each side of the Black Eagle.

Lars flicked off the comm, disconnecting them from the Defiance ship. "I'm guessing those aren't enemy ships, based on the smile on your face."

"Those aren't even ships," said Eddie proudly.

Lars stared at the vessel just in front of the Black Eagle. "Huh? They *look* like ships."

"Holograms are funny like that," said Eddie.

"Holograms?" sputtered Lars. "Strong Arm, are you doing that?"

Julianna answered right away. "Yes, they're projections. After the right modifications, Hatch was able to make them appear as actual ships on the radar too. Just one of many upgrades to this Omega-line Q-Ship."

"Damn, that's remarkable," said Lars.

"Looks like it's time to bring this guy in," said Eddie. "Finally."

"Finally?" questioned Julianna. "This took a whole five minutes—you're so impatient. But yes, let's bring him in and end this."

Lars nodded, flipping the comm switch. "Defiance, we're sending out tow cables. Cooperate, and you will not be harmed."

There was no reply as Eddie fed out the cables and locked them securely into place. After they had been reinforced, Eddie signaled Julianna. "Strong Arm, we're all set. Meet you back at *ArchAngel*."

The Q-Ship projections disappeared from around the Black Eagle. "Copy," responded Julianna. "I'll be waiting with a welcome gift for our guest."

"Freshly baked muffins?" asked Eddie, mock hope in his voice.

"With fucking crumble on top," said Julianna.

4

Loading Bay, QBS *ArchAngel*, Lorialis System

Julianna aimed a rifle at the rogue Black Eagle's airlock as the ship slid to a halt in the landing bay, and the crew sprinted in like a well-oiled machine, chaining the craft down to the dock at once.

Julianna eyed the weapon in her hands. It was, sadly, more obsolete than the decommissioned ship in front of her.

I'm getting new weapons soon, she thought, turning the gun over and examining its side.

That could link you all to the Federation, Pip warned.

Not if I steal them from some pirates.

You'd better find the richest pirates you can, or their weapons won't be any better than what you currently have.

Fighting undercover for the Federation had its perks, one of them being that they didn't have to follow the same protocols as other divisions. However, the outdated weapons were a definite downside.

The crew had peeled back a safe distance and waited in silence.

Eddie and Lars were stationed in front of the ship's hatch when it finally cracked open.

"Hold your fire and wait for my command," said Julianna. She stepped forward, trying to get a good look at the pilot.

The cockpit door rose several more centimeters before she could see the pilot's face, and she realized that he was human. By the time the man was in full view he had raised his hands above his head, and his eyes darted between her rifle and the other crew members.

"I surrender! I surrender! I surrender!" the guy said, his voice frantic as he stared down the barrel of Julianna's gun. He was in his early twenties, about like Chester, but had a black Mohawk and green eyes. A silver metal ring looped through his eyebrow and he had another piercing in the ear on the opposite side.

"Step down slowly," Julianna ordered, motioning to the floor with her rifle.

The pilot, who seemed more like a kid than anything with his pale face and shaking hands, did exactly as he was told. He dropped to his knees, keeping his hands behind his head. Julianna motioned to Lars. "Search him. And don't try anything stupid," she told the boy. "We like to shoot first and ask questions later around here."

The guy's face tightened when Lars reached into his waistband and pulled out a pistol which looked somehow more obsolete than the weapons they'd been using on this ship.

"I thought you said you didn't mean me any harm," the stranger said.

"We don't," said Julianna with a smile, the rifle in her hands steady, "but we need to ensure you're the peaceful sort. We heard you mention the Brotherhood. Are you working for them?"

The man's mouth fell open. "Fuck, no! I'm *running* from them."

"Why's that?" asked Eddie, stepping closer to Julianna as Lars drew back, raising his own weapon.

The kid started speaking quickly, obviously scared. "Defiance, the trading company I worked with, they were selling weapons to the Brotherhood. Well, actually they were selling guns to a human the Brotherhood appeared to be working for, someone named 'Felix Castile.'"

"Okay, good. Now we're getting somewhere," said Julianna.

"I'd been on a run for Mateo," continued the pilot. "I wasn't there when they did the trade. I showed up…" The guy's eyes shot to his knees, then to his side. They darted all over, but they didn't focus on anything. They were frantic, almost like he was seeing something…or reliving it.

Julianna had seen this many times—this kid was in shock—and she lowered her weapon. "What did you see? What happened?" she asked, her voice a bit softer.

"He… The Brotherhood… They killed *everyone*. The entire Defiance Trading Company is dead," he said, his eyes jerking from side to side.

Eddie's gaze connected with Julianna's and he gave her

a slight nod, then lowered his rifle as well. "No, they didn't, since *you're* still alive." Eddie turned to Lars, who was still held his rifle at the ready. "Will you please lead our visitor to an interrogation room?"

Julianna stepped forward, motioning for the stranger to lower his hands. "We call it an interrogation room, but please try to understand that we only want to talk. It sounds like we have mutual enemies. We can help you."

A tremor ran over the boy's face but he nodded, getting to his feet as Lars approached him. The Kezzin led him through the bay door, with Eddie and Julianna following closely behind.

The lights in the interrogation room were low, causing the Defiance pilot to squint at the pair when they entered.

"What's your name, son?" asked Eddie, perching on the edge of the table and gazing down at him.

"Knox Gunnerson," he said, looking at Eddie and Julianna quizzically. "Are you with the Federation?"

Julianna shook their head. "No, we're a rogue outfit about like the Defiance Trading Company, but we don't sell weapons to terrorists. We spend our energy and resources trying to stop the terrorists that your organization supplies."

"The Defiance Trading Company isn't bad. We're—well, we used to be—there to help the little guy, help those who needed to defend themselves. It isn't easy to get your hands on artillery out on the fringe. It's different there. You wouldn't understand." Knox lowered his eyes to the table, cold resolve settling in them.

"I think we *would* understand," said Eddie, his voice calm. "Our job is to stop these terrorists—the same people who took out your company. If you help us, maybe we can find them before they hurt anyone else."

"What weapons did your people sell them?" asked Julianna.

Knox pursed his lips, looking like he was suddenly unwilling to talk.

"Look," said Julianna, "we know how desperate things have gotten for some, and we're not blaming you for what's happened. We're just trying to make sense of it. Will you help us?" She pulled out a chair and took a seat, hoping it made her appear less intimidating.

"I've been with the company for a while, ever since my pops disappeared. It's hard surviving out there on your own, you know?" Knox ran his hand over his Mohawk, making it fall and bounce back slightly.

"I think we do." Eddie held out a hand. "I'm Captain Eddie Teach, and I promise I know *exactly* how hard it is to be alone out here."

Knox eyed the hand, but didn't take it. Instead, his gaze swept to Julianna.

Reading the question in his eyes, she said, "I'm Commander Julianna Fregin."

"And you're all trying to defend against people like the Brotherhood?" asked Knox, then quickly added, "You know it's impossible. They're too big and too powerful, especially now."

Julianna took in a steadying breath. She didn't think

this guy was bad. Scared, but not bad—there was a big difference. "I think we'd all be a bit happier if you could list exactly what the Brotherhood took from Defiance. We know you've been through a lot and we'd like to offer you safety here on the ship, but we need—"

"Safety in the brig, right?" challenged Knox.

"Well, we don't actually *know* you," began Eddie. "Until we have more information—"

"They took it all," Knox burst out, looking frantic. "They took our whole armory, including six mini-nukes."

Eddie cast a quick look at Julianna, who kept her eyes on Knox. Nukes were strictly illegal in the Federation, so the notion that their enemy had acquired some was alarming, to say the least.

"You said Felix Castile was there. What else can you tell us about him?" asked Julianna.

"We don't sell to just anyone. Commander Lytes, I believe it was, got Castile in contact with Mateo. I wouldn't have even known about it, but the call came while we were working on my ship together," explained Knox. He stood and began pacing, looking down at the floor like a rush of emotion was about to burst from him, then halted and brought his scared eyes to Eddie like he didn't know what to say next.

"Go on, son. What happened?" urged Eddie.

Knox swallowed and resumed pacing. "We—Defiance, I mean—don't deal with anyone we don't know. We don't want to get blown to bits, you know." He laughed coldly. "I guess we dropped the ball on that, since most everyone was killed. Anyway, Mateo said he wouldn't deal with Felix even though Commander Lytes vouched for him. That was when Felix offered another reference that Mateo trusted, someone on Ronin he knew well. A trustworthy client."

"You think this guy was lying?" asked Julianna.

Knox shook his head. "I think this Felix person intimidated him. Axel has never lied to us before, and he had no reason to ruin relations with the Defiance. I trust him."

"Will you give us more information on this Axel person? Can we find him on Ronin?" asked Eddie.

Knox shrugged. "I could, but I doubt he'd talk to you. If I'm right, he's not going to trust anyone he doesn't know—not after what Felix did."

Eddie twisted his lips, disappointed.

"What if..." Julianna began. "What if you established contact for us? Set up a meeting? If you know this Axel person..."

"Axel Link," supplied Knox, "and yes, I've gone on a few runs to Ronin to supply him. He trusts me. Well, as much as he trusts anyone."

Eddie's eyes looked renewed with excitement. "That's great! If you can make contact with him, we may find a clue as to where Felix is hiding."

Knox looked unsure and chewed the inside of his cheek.

Eddie could sympathize with his uncertainty. "We need to find out as much about Felix Castile and the Brotherhood as we can so we can take them down. Do you want to be part of that?"

Knox paused for a long moment before he nodded slowly and answered, "Yeah. Yeah, I think I do. I'd love to watch those assholes pay."

5

Jack Renfro's Office, QBS *ArchAngel*, Behemoth System

Jack and Julianna were engaged in what sounded like a heated discussion when Eddie entered the office and he paused to study the two. They in turn stopped conversing to look at him.

"If this is about the crate of Blue Ale that disappeared, I've got no leads," said Eddie, taking a seat next to Julianna.

Jack shook his head. "We stopped wondering about any missing alcohol after you joined."

Eddie winked. "Good call. I support that line of thinking."

Julianna pushed back in her chair, swiveling her chiseled and serious jaw in Eddie's direction. "Jack seems to think that Knox should accompany us to meet with Axel Link."

"That's a great idea!" Eddie said. His tone surprising Julianna, who reacted with revulsion. Seeing her face,

Eddie shook his head. "A great idea for a *crazy* person, I mean."

Jack, always good-tempered, folded his hands on the top of his desk and gazed at them calmly. "I totally understand the Commander's concerns about this Knox Gunnerson person—he's a potential hazard to this crew and our mission—but I've checked out his records, and can attest that so far everything he's told you adds up. Looks like his father went missing a long time ago, leaving him to fend for himself on the streets. He has no crimes on his record, and he's tested negative for any narcotics."

"You had him tested?" Eddie pushed forward in his seat, alarmed.

"We don't know anything about him," Jack explained.

"We didn't know anything about Lars either," retorted Eddie.

"But Lars saved our asses," Julianna cut in.

"Give this guy half a chance and he might do the same. He's a fucking orphan." Eddie didn't know why he was so outraged, except that he felt sympathy for the boy. Knox had been labeled as a criminal automatically, it seemed, which gave him zero chance at redemption unless someone believed in him and gave him the opportunity to prove himself.

Julianna frowned. "Teach, you want to adopt a bunch of puppies, do it on your own time. We have to be careful who we bring on this ship. We can't let our guard down for just anyone."

Jack cut in with, "Understandably the Commander is worried about Knox going on this mission, but I think that pairing her caution with your openness is the perfect balance. Knox could be a live wire, or he could be exactly who we need to fill in a missing piece in the puzzle concerning Felix. We need something—anything!—that will tell us what he's planning."

"We know that he has a personal vendetta against General Reynolds for something that happened long ago."

He was holding a grudge. That was all they knew about Felix Castile. The General had told them that he'd personally brief them on the history later. What was important now was getting a step ahead of Felix and cutting him off before he did too much damage.

Chewing angrily on her lip, Julianna nodded. "I agree with that. Felix has an army now, and it's bigger than before. If this Axel Link person knows something or someone with information, it could be the intel we need to solve this puzzle."

"Knox said he had Axel's trust," stated Jack, "which means you're going to need him to get there. From what I can tell from reviewing the intel we have, Axel won't talk to just anyone." Jack tapped a pad on his desk, one that apparently contained all the information the Federation possessed on Axel. "He's a retired weaponsmith, and is supposedly highly paranoid. He's rumored to be holed up in a heavily-guarded old building somewhere on Ronin. You said Knox made runs there for Defiance, correct?"

"That was what he said," answered Eddie, trying to read the contents of the pad as Jack pushed it toward them.

"Then I think the boy needs to go with you, especially because of the location," said Jack.

"The location?" asked Julianna just as the door opened behind them.

Hatch, who was absentmindedly paging through notes on a pad he was holding in one of his tentacles, hardly looked up as he entered. Only then did Eddie realize that the chair on the other side of Julianna had been specially designed for Hatch.

"Yes. The location is why I've invited Doctor A'Din Hatcherik to join us." Jack offered a hand to the Londil, who took a seat in the modified chair. His tentacles found resting places on the many different arms.

Hatch paused a moment to adjust before looking at Eddie. "Gun Barrel. That's the city in which this weapon-smith lives."

"Do you know him?" asked Julianna, leaning forward.

"Link? Oh, no. I've heard of him, though. He used to be a big deal in the weapons trade." Eyes still resting on Eddie, Hatch continued, "You better be prepared, because Gun Barrel ain't for the faint of heart. It's a tough place, Teach. Make one dumb move and you'll get yourself blown up."

"Doctor A'Din Hatcherik, you said there was something you could offer us," urged Jack.

"ArchAngel or Pip can give you facts on Gun Barrel. You can and should listen to them," said Hatch as the monitor on the wall behind Jack flickered to life.

"Did I hear my name?" asked ArchAngel, her face appearing on the display.

"You didn't," Hatch said, puffing out his cheeks and looking annoyed.

"I do believe that you said I should be listened to. Does that mean you count me as a resource?" asked ArchAngel, sounding amused.

"I *believe* we are having a meeting," said Hatch, looking away sharply.

Eddie regarded the AI, and then Hatch. "I guess you two are having a bit of a spat. Seems like that kind of thing is bound to happen when you share a ship."

"Doctor A'Din Hatcherik prefers Pip over me, that's all. He would rather wait around for Pip to help and not get a project done than rely on anyone else," ArchAngel informed them.

"What? What does she mean?" asked Julianna.

"She means that her software is fried and needs to be deleted. I just find Pip to be more in line with my personality, that's all. It's kind of like Teach and me—we simply don't get along," said Hatch.

"I love the hell out of you. What are you talking about?" asked Eddie, goading the mechanic.

Julianna stroked her chin with her thumb. "Oh. Well, I guess I can understand having preferences, but still, ArchAngel is part of our team... Julianna's voice trailed off and she had a strange expression on her face. She hadn't been the same since Pip had become sentient. Eddie was going to get to the bottom of that—whatever was going on with her—one way or another.

Jack cleared his throat and everyone looked at him, suddenly remembering why they were there. "Right. Doctor, you were saying?"

Hatch wrapped two tentacles around the pad in front of him. "I was saying that Teach would die in Gun Barrel, but what I'd like to elaborate on is that there are both climate issues and a dress code. You won't survive long in that city without minding both."

"The climate?" asked Julianna.

Hatch tapped the screen and then began reading. "At any given time, the winds can be upward of thirty miles per hour."

"That's not too bad. I've been in way worse," said Eddie.

"Except this is the dry desert, and the city is prone to dust storms. Have you ever seen one of *those?*" asked Hatch. He looked smug, like he knew the answer was going to be no.

"If I did, then I slept through it," teased Eddie.

Hatch shot right back at him, "Well, a dust storm offers zero visibility and can suffocate you within a minute."

"Can you make us a dust-storm suit?" asked Eddie.

"I could, but you'd be shot on the spot," said Hatch with finality.

Eddie jabbed his elbow playfully in Julianna's direction. "I vote for no dust-storm suit, then. What do you say?"

"You mentioned a dress code?" asked Julianna.

Hatch puffed his cheeks. "Yes. This town was modeled after the old West on Earth, which fits the climate. There's a main road, a saloon, horses, and a slew of cowboys."

"Cow-what?" asked Eddie, a wide grin forming on his face. He thought Hatch was kidding, but the look on the doctor's quickly deflating cheeks told him otherwise.

"Cow*boys*. If you hope to stroll through that town and not get shot immediately you're going to need new clothes, something that won't make you stick out," explained Hatch.

"Knox goes there, so why can't we dress like him?" asked Eddie.

"Have you *looked* at the boy? He doesn't look anything like you two in your uniforms," said Hatch.

"So we need torn-up clothes and a funky haircut?" asked Eddie.

"That would make you look like riffraff. You want to look superior enough that you don't get everyone and their dog riled up. If you have the whole town shooting at you, you won't make it out alive," said Hatch.

"But if we blend in?" asked Julianna.

"Then you'll stroll in there without a problem," conceded Hatch. "You can find Axel and stroll out without being questioned."

"So what do we need to do, and what do we need to wear?" asked Julianna.

Hatch spun the pad in his tentacles to face them. It showed a picture of a man wearing blue jeans, a crisscross-patterned shirt, and a Stetson hat. "You're going to have to dress like cowboys."

6

Rooming Corridor, QBS *ArchAngel*, Behemoth System

Eddie nodded to the guard outside Knox's room. Julianna might have been right that he belonged in the brig, but Eddie just couldn't sanction that. Instead they compromised, and a guard was stationed outside his room around the clock.

"At ease," he said when the guard saluted.

Eddie pulled a beer out of the case he'd brought and handed it to the guard. "For you," he said, then added, "when you're off-duty, of course."

"Uh, yes, sir. Thank you," said the guard, taking the beer with an awkward smile. He pressed a button on the wall, and the door to Knox's room slid back to show him lying on his bed, hands clasped over his abdomen and eyes pinned on the ceiling.

"Hey there," said Eddie, plopping the case of Blue Ale on the floor between the stiff chair and the bed. The room wasn't cozy, but it was definitely adequate. Eddie had certainly stayed in worse conditions—*way* worse. He suspected Knox had too.

"Did you come to see if I was plotting to take over your ship?" asked Knox, his tone dull and bored.

"Not *my* ship, just borrowing it as a base of operations for the time being." Eddie popped the top off the beer using a churchkey and took a sip. "And no. I think you're a pretty resourceful guy, but I don't think you'd stand a chance of taking over this ship on your best day. No offense."

"Oh yeah?" asked Knox, sitting up. He eyed the case of beer before looking at Eddie.

"Go on, I brought them for you. Well, for me too. Okay, I mostly brought them for me, since I'm guessing you're a lightweight." Eddie laughed, giving the kid an easy smile.

Knox started to smirk, but stopped himself and grabbed a beer, although he didn't open it. "I might be able to take this ship. You don't know."

"Yeah? Watch this," said Eddie. He cleared his throat. "ArchAngel?"

"Yes, Eddie? What do you need?" asked ArchAngel's voice overhead.

Knox's eyes widened in alarm as the AI spoke, causing Eddie to show a slight smile.

"Who flies this ship?" asked Eddie.

"I do, of course," answered ArchAngel.

"Can anyone take control from you, even someone who is quite resourceful?" challenged Eddie.

"All scenarios predict that to be impossible, so, no. This will remain my ship," said ArchAngel, "indefinitely."

"Thanks, ArchAngel. That's all I wanted to know."

Eddie took another drink and leaned back in the chair, crossing his feet on the floor.

"If you're not worried about me taking over the ship, then what's with the guard?" asked Knox.

Eddie shrugged. "Just a precaution. I wouldn't worry about it."

Knox used the key to open his own beer and tossed it on the table beside the bed, holding the beverage up slightly in Eddie's direction as if in gratitude. "Was that an AI? I've heard about those, but I've never met one before."

"Sure was," said Eddie, taking another pull.

"You must have stolen this ship from the Federation then," Knox deduced.

Eddie didn't correct him, just sipped his beer and studied the boy. He was young, yet had wisdom in his eyes. It must have been all those years of living on the fringe. Hardship in all its many forms often made for clever men.

After a moment Knox said, "Why are you being so nice to me?"

Eddie shrugged like he wasn't quite sure, even though he knew full well the reason. "We need you to take us directly to Axel instead of just arranging the meeting."

Knox didn't seem shocked by the suggestion. "I was planning to do that...if it turned out you weren't a bunch of assholes. Axel doesn't allow any visitors in to see him except me. He'd smell something fishy if I set up a meeting. Not really the trusting type, I guess."

"Yeah?" asked Eddie.

Knox nodded. "He shoots trespassers, but usually doesn't kill them unless he has to."

"So, in one scenario you were going to allow us to walk in there and get ourselves shot?" asked Eddie, amused.

"That would only have happened if you were assholes." Knox held up the beer. "But you brought me a beer and honestly, so far you guys seem all right. A bit on the edgy side, but who on the fringe isn't? I just haven't figured out if I can trust you yet."

"Same here, but my instinct tells me I can," agreed Eddie. He was watching Knox study the room, but suspected he was mostly putting things together in his brain. Knox was smart, and eventually he'd figure out what Eddie and Julianna were doing out here. It was only a matter of time.

"That ship of yours," began Eddie. "The Black Eagle. Where did you get it?"

Knox smiled, his eyes a little distant as if he were remembering. "*Catfish*—that's what I nicknamed her. Mateo gave her to me, let me paint her."

Eddie remembered the immature whiskers and fin spray painted on the side of the ship. It gave the vessel personality—about like Knox.

"Mateo was in charge of the Defiance Trading Company, right?" Eddie's tone shifted. He knew Mateo had died. Worse, he knew Knox had watched it happen. Now, hearing this kid speak of his former boss like this, it sounded like Mateo had been more than just the boy's employer. A mentor, or perhaps even a father?

Knox nodded. "Yeah, but he wasn't a bad guy, I can tell you that much." His tone grew defensive, like he expected accusations to follow. The boy's walls were going up again.

Eddie took a long drink and belched. "I didn't say he was."

"Well, I get that it was a shifty operation. He wouldn't have sold guns to Felix under normal circumstances, but we needed the money. Things were changing. Deals had dried up recently."

"It's because there are other groups doing what Defiance did. Groups operating inside Federation space," explained Eddie. "How'd you get mixed up with them anyway? You mentioned your father before."

Knox took a quick drink to cover his expression and wiped his hand across his mouth. "Yeah, after my pops disappeared I didn't have anywhere to go. I was just a kid then." His voice trailed off, memories reflected in his eyes. Eddie found it amusing that Knox thought he had been just a kid back in those days. He still looked like a teenager even now.

Knox cleared his throat and continued, "I was living on the streets trying not to starve to death, and every day I'd line up for rations from the Food Bank. It wasn't much, just a slice of bread usually, but I'd get my rations and go off to eat. I didn't like to cram it all in my mouth at once like the other kids did, because once it's gone, it's gone. You learn to save some of it, even just the crumbs."

Eddie nodded but said nothing.

Knox took another swig. "I was about to take my first bite when something slammed into the back of my head. I still remember the shock of it. The confusion. I fell to the ground and my bread dropped into a dirty puddle. There was blood running down my neck, but all I could think about was how my bread was ruined. Can you imagine that?" He laughed, surprising Eddie, then shook his head. "Anyway, I rolled over and saw some bigger kids towering over me. They were pissed that I'd dropped the bread, since that was the whole reason they were there in the first place. They started beating me, one after the next, pinning me down so I couldn't fight back, until a voice yelled for them to stop. They ran off when they saw it was a grown man and he was heading our way. I pushed myself up and tried to stand, but then I saw the one who had yelled at us. He was huge, like he'd never gone a day without eating a mountain of protein. You want to talk about terrifying? He had a long scar over his eye, and snarled when he got to me. I thought he was going to kill me." Knox laughed again, a fond look on his face.

"What happened next?" asked Eddie.

"He yelled at me. Can you believe that? He yelled at me right after I got my ass beaten." Knox took in a big breath and puffed out his cheeks, his voice suddenly much deeper. "What the hell is wrong with you, kid? You can't just sit there like that! You need to stand up! Fight back!" Knox looked up at Eddie with a smile, but let it quickly fade into a frown. He pushed off the bed and exchanged an empty bottle for a full one.

Eddie realized he still had half a beer, so maybe this guy *could* outdrink him after all. "That was Mateo?"

Knox nodded. "Yeah. He took me in and cleaned me up to start with, but then he taught me how to fight and he gave me my first pistol. Later he taught me how to fly. Not anything professional like how you all flew those ships... He just taught me the basics, but it was enough for me to start with. After we pulled that Black Eagle, he started teaching me how to fix her. We'd been working on her for a few months when the deal went down and…" The smile on Knox's face had vanished and now there was only the grief and anger. The expression had appeared quickly after the end of the story, and it made his eyes narrow with pain. "I've never had much, but now I have nothing and it's all because of Felix and the Brotherhood. I wanted to kill them when I saw what they did. I wanted to mow them down."

"I would have felt the same way," Eddie agreed.

Knox deflated. "I ran away instead like a fucking weakling. What would Mateo have said if he had seen me doing that?"

Eddie shook his head. "He would have said that you were smart. You were outnumbered, but you're alive to tell the tale. Sometimes you fight, but sometimes you run so you can fight another day."

Knox nodded reluctantly. "I did manage to shoot two Brotherhood soldiers on my way out."

"Did you kill them?" asked Eddie.

"Nah. I guess I could have, but Mateo had always taught me that if you didn't have to kill someone you shouldn't. I just disabled them."

"You must be a pretty good shot to pull that off," said Eddie, impressed. Going for the chest was the easy option.

"Axel taught me to shoot. That was why Mateo made it so I was the only one who did his runs. He'd always take an hour to help me train whenever I stopped by." There was a new lightness in Knox's eyes now, the anger suddenly gone. "You'll like Axel. He's a good guy, about like how

Mateo was. Gritty as hell, but I think that's part of the charm."

"Mateo sounds like he was good at his core," said Eddie, giving him a kind smile.

"I never much cared for what we did at Defiance, but I was indebted to Mateo so I did what he told me to do. He might have supplied criminals, but he wasn't one of them. I know that's not enough to justify his actions, but…"

"I've done some pretty questionable things in my past," said Eddie. "Many out there are just trying to survive, like Mateo and his crew. However, when I had the means to do better, I tried to do better things. That's what you have to ask yourself right now… Are you ready to do better?"

"I'm ready to bring down those assholes. I've seen enough to know that bullying others in an arms war is reckless. They all want the bigger gun, and it never ends. I'm fucking tired of bullies," said Knox with real venom in his tone.

"I couldn't agree with you more," said Eddie, taking a long sip.

The two men continued to drink long into the night.

7

Omega-line Q-Ship, Gun Barrel, Planet Ronin, Behemoth System

Knox watched Eddie as he checked the radar.

Julianna kept peering at the boy. It wasn't that she didn't trust him so much as she had trouble *reading* him. He appeared to have a natural curiosity, which meant he catalogued everything he observed. It was a quality not many people shared or even noticed, but this boy seemed to possess it—and that was something to be watched.

"These fucking boots pinch my toes," Julianna said as she flew the Q-Ship closer to the surface. The land was brown, mostly, a long stretch of desert bordered by mountains.

"Over there is the town." Eddie pointed to two rows of shanty buildings with roofs covered in piles of dust and dirt. "Is that the building where Axel is located?" he asked Knox, referring to a barnlike structure on the south side of town.

"That's it," Knox confirmed.

"Doesn't look like such a big deal," said Eddie, blowing out a breath. "I kind of agree about the boots, and this shirt is pretty scratchy too." He pulled at the collared button-up shirt he wore that had red, white, and blue stripes.

"And it provides zero protection, so try not to get shot," said Julianna with a commiserating look. She was wearing jeans and a flannel shirt as well.

"Wasn't that why we dressed in this get up? To avoid getting shot?" asked Eddie.

"You'll blend in with the locals," Knox offered. "Mostly."

Eddie spun around. "Mostly?"

"Well, your clothes look pretty new," Knox observed. "That's not usually the case in Gun Barrel, due to the dust storms."

Eddie nodded slowly. "That makes sense. I'll roll around in the dirt once we get there." His eyes drifted to the window and he watched the sun as it towered over the horizon, beating its heat against the town. "Why do they call it 'Gun Barrel,' anyway?"

"Because the main road is as straight as a gun barrel," explained Knox.

Eddie pursed his lips. "Huh."

"What a literal place," said Julianna. She had Pip cloak the ship before she landed it behind some caves on the north end of town. This area was significantly less populated, so it was the obvious choice. She couldn't help but notice that Knox was observing her and took in everything she did, so for the second time today she noted how inquisitive he was.

Eddie got to his feet once the ship had settled. "Yee-haw! Who's ready for a hootenanny?"

Julianna sank back, giving Eddie her trademark, "What the hell is wrong with you" expression. "*What* did you just say?"

"Yee—"

"I heard what you said, but where did you learn it?" asked Julianna.

"I saw a special on the Earth's Old West. I kind of get why Gun Barrel chose to model their town after it. Cowboys were awesome." Eddie picked something up from the other side of his chair—a cowboy hat, which he placed on his head.

Without a doubt he looked like a tourist, or maybe a cartoon character. Julianna and Knox started laughing.

"We're trying *not* to draw attention to ourselves. Blend in, remember?" Julianna said. She pulled a handkerchief from her pocket. Currently the winds were low, but she'd heard that could change dramatically at any moment.

"I *am* blending in. Don't they wear cowboy hats like this?" Eddie asked.

Knox nodded. "Actually they do, but that hat makes your head look big and it is obviously brand new. It hasn't been worn in. Most of these people have been wearing the same hat for years, maybe decades."

"First of all, I can't help it if my head is big. I've just got a huge brain," said Eddie, pulling his hat lower.

"Yeah, that's it," said Julianna. She rolled her eyes, but smiled.

"And second," continued Eddie, "this was my only

option. It wasn't like we had a worn-out Stetson just sitting around. I had to act fast."

"Fair enough, but that doesn't change the fact that you look silly," teased Julianna. She opened the back hatch and took a look at the oppressive desert that stretched before them, then stepped out and walked some distance from the cloaked ship so she wouldn't give its placement away should anyone happen upon them.

After the group had gone several meters beyond the perimeter of the cloak Knox looked behind him, only to jerk back. "Whoa, the ship disappeared!" he exclaimed. "Where did it go?"

When Julianna turned Eddie shot her a big wink and spun to face Knox, his arms out in alarm. "What? What did you do with it, Knox? You were the last one to step out."

The color drained from Knox's face. "I promise I didn't do anything. I just followed you!"

Eddie looked at Julianna with a serious expression on his face. "Do you think he hit the D-button on his way out?"

Julianna agreed with a nod. "It appears so."

"Great, now we're stuck forever on this planet. Damn it, Knox, never step on the D-button!" Eddie groaned in feigned frustration and shook his head.

Knox's frightened expression diminished as he stared at where the ship had been and then at Eddie. Something was computing. He slowly walked back to where the ship had landed and reached out to touch its invisible surface, understanding dawning on his face. "The ship is—"

"Cloaked," supplied Julianna. "And you're right, Eddie's

a real jerk. You'll find it strangely endearing...maybe. That's what I hear from the crew, anyway."

"Aw shucks, Jules," said Eddie drawled. "I hope one day you're endeared as hell to me. It would swell my cowboy heart."

"I think I'm going to puke on my boots," said Julianna, and ambled toward the main road. The other two laughed as they followed her.

The road wound at first but finally straightened, just as Knox had described. Brown buildings bordered both sides, and it seemed to go on well into the horizon. Julianna stopped to survey the last stretch.

Eddie halted at her side with his hand resting on the pistol in his holster and peered out from under his cowboy hat, squinting and measuring up the town. It appeared quiet. A bit *too* quiet.

A tumbleweed rolled out from between two squatty buildings, continuing straight across the road and knocking into a pair of posts with a couple brown horses tied to them. A sign above the building read Saloon.

Eddie's mouth pulled to the side, and he looked at Julianna as if he were asking permission.

"No," she said plainly.

"But don't you want to taste their version of whiskey or bathtub bourbon or whatever their specialty is?" he asked.

"Their specialty is death to your insides. You don't want the drinks here," Knox cut in. Then he swiveled his head over his shoulder, looking unnerved. "Something isn't right. There should be more people out right now, since the winds haven't kicked up yet."

"What do you mean?" asked Julianna.

"I think we better get out of here," said Knox, glancing in the direction of the ship. He looked scared. Focused, but scared.

Eddie kept his attention on the long main road, but reached out and placed a hand on Knox's shoulder. "We aren't backing out now, kid. We've come all this way. Stay close to us." He looked at Julianna for confirmation, and she tipped her head.

They strode forward, sand and small pebbles crunching under their boots. In a nearby window of the General Store Julianna spotted an older woman, but she ducked the moment their eyes met. That couldn't be a good sign.

Aerial surveillance scans complete, said Pip.

Please take your time with any updates. I don't get the impression at all that we're being watched by an enemy, Julianna replied, her tone overflowing with sarcasm. She flexed her fingers over her pistol as they moved forward.

Don't worry, the locals all appear to be inside.

Because?

Because there are six Brotherhood soldiers stationed around Axel's building.

Julianna skirted over to the opposite side of the road from where Axel's building stood and Eddie followed at once, taking his cue from her crouched position. Without Julianna having said a word, he sensed her caution.

They're camouflaged to blend in, unlike you in your plaid shirts.

Hindsight, thought Julianna.

She stopped moving when she reached a trough roughly three buildings down from Axel's place.

"You wanna tell us what's going on?" asked Eddie,

sinking beside her and looking over his shoulder. He kept his head low.

"The Brotherhood are here, six soldiers on Axel's building. I'm getting positions now," she said.

"Dammit, they beat us here," hissed Eddie.

"Brotherhood? How do you know that?" asked Knox, staring at the empty road.

"She has Pip in her head," explained Eddie, retrieving his second pistol from his left ankle.

"Pip?" asked Knox.

"He's an AI," said Eddie. He handed Knox the gun. "Take this and watch your ass."

Julianna held up two fingers and pointed to the roof, then indicated two more soldiers on either side of the building. Eddie, understanding at once, nodded. She pointed to another trough roughly twenty yards down the street.

When she had received confirmation, she ducked and sprinted down the wooden boards of the sidewalk. The gunfire started immediately and dogged her footsteps, nearly catching her boot several times.

She jammed her back to the trough and waited for the pause in the gunfire. In unison she and Eddie sprang to their feet and fired over their respective troughs, Julianna shooting at the north end of the building and Eddie toward the roof. She saw Knox using the weapon Eddie had supplied in her peripheral vision.

Two Brotherhood soldiers fell from the top of the building and another dropped flat onto his chest from the alley's shadow with a bullet in his forehead.

Julianna slid back behind the trough and reloaded,

taking steadying breaths. When she finished, she lifted up enough to survey the scene: Three bodies, not a bad start.

A moment later Eddie and Knox ran to her position, crouching to avoid enemy fire.

Eddie slammed into the wall beside her breathing heavily, sweat on his face. The two exchanged a look as he reloaded his pistol, and he grinned. "What do you think, did we nail them all?"

It would appear so, but you might have one playing possum, suggested Pip.

Did you just make that reference?

I believe I did.

I don't think I even know you anymore.

Or are you just starting to really know me?

Why don't you make yourself useful and download all available data from the network drive once we're inside?

Did you mean to say please?

I did, with all my heart.

She shook her head. "Pip says we *might* be in the clear. You take the south end and I'll take the north."

He nodded, lifting his pistol parallel with his cheek.

Soundlessly, guns at the ready, the veteran soldiers slid out from behind the trough, and Knox trailed Eddie. His form wasn't bad, Julianna noted, observing his posture and how his eyes meticulously scanned.

She fetched up against a building with boarded-over windows and toed the body of the Kezzin in the opening of the alleyway, which didn't budge. After a short breath she slid out, ready to shoot, but the alleyway was empty. There had been two soldiers here so Julianna looked up, her gun following her gaze.

From Eddie's relaxed demeanor she guessed the other two targets were dead, so she jogged over to him. Two Brotherhood soldiers lay in front of the building, and two more reposed in the alleyway.

"We've got one missing," Julianna informed them.

"Then he'll be *that* way," said Eddie, pointing to the back of the building.

Pip, did you see which way he went?

I didn't. He disappeared before I could track him. Backing up footage now, but the Brotherhood soldiers are wearing special equipment to avoid detection, as I said before.

"Shall I lead the way?" Julianna asked her two companions.

Eddie shook his head, then pointed toward the opposite end of the alley where the dead Kezzin was lying on the ground. Without another word Julianna nodded, letting him know that she understood.

She raised her gun and walked backward, scanning the rooftop and the opening of the alleyway, then paused and listened to the sounds of this place. Air whistling. Old wooden boards creaking. Heavy breathing, but not hers or Eddie's. There was someone else here.

A gun cocked.

Julianna opened her eyes and whipped around. "Eddie, move—"

The soldier came out of the alley ahead of Julianna and fired.

Julianna slid to the opposite wall and shot back at the enemy soldier. He returned it, but then took Julianna's shot directly in the head and collapsed.

His bullet missed her, whizzing by her head and going farther into the alley.

"No!" yelled Knox. In a swift movement he pushed Eddie out of the line of fire, knocking him to the ground and covering him with his body.

"Fuck!" exclaimed Eddie, pushing himself up and rubbing the back of his head. "That'll leave a mark."

Knox staggered to his feet beside Eddie. He cupped his bicep and there was blood on his fingers when he pulled them away.

Julianna ran to the boy's side. "You've been shot!"

Eddie's eyes widened when he saw the wound. "Knox!"

"It just grazed. S-sorry," said the former gunrunner. "I should've been faster."

"What the hell were you thinking, man?" asked Eddie, holstering his gun and gently taking Knox's arm to look at the wound.

"He was thinking about saving you," said Julianna, surprised and relieved at the same time.

8

Gun Barrel, Planet Ronin, Behemoth System

Eddie yanked the bandana off his neck and tied it around Knox's arm. "Are you all right?" he asked, grateful that Julianna was guarding them so he could tend to Knox.

Although breathless, Knox nodded. "It went through. I'll be okay. I think."

Eddie frowned. "What were you thinking, pushing me out of the way? You could have gotten yourself killed."

"If I hadn't you would've been shot," answered Knox.

Eddie stared at the spot he'd been standing in, which was squarely in the middle of the alleyway. The bullet would have hit him, no doubt about it. He could've even died.

Eddie tied the bandana tightly, making Knox grimace with pain. It was for the best, since they needed to stop the bleeding. "Just don't make this a habit, okay? You let me handle it next time."

"Hopefully there won't *be* a next time," said Knox weakly.

"There always is," said Eddie, pulling his gun back out of his holster. He turned to Julianna, who was still on guard and scanning the area. "What does Pip think?"

"That you're lucky as hell," said Julianna, glancing at the wound in Knox's arm and then at Eddie. There was a new expression in her eyes he hadn't seen before. Did she look relieved? Relieved he hadn't taken a bullet to the chest? "And he says we're clear, as far as he can tell."

Eddie blew out a sigh of relief and turned toward the rear alley. "No more pushing yourself, Gunner," he said to Knox. "Take it easy for the rest of this trip."

Knox laughed despite a bit of pain. "Sure, I get ya."

Eddie flattened himself against the wooden building when they neared the end and looked at the space across from the structure, checking that all was clear. Then he spun around, gun out, to ensure no more soldiers were in hiding.

"Up there," said Knox, pointing to a set of stairs at the back of the building that led to the second floor.

Eddie took the lead again, listening for waiting Brotherhood soldiers at each step.

"Oh, fuck," said Julianna.

Eddie saw what her enhanced vision had already discerned. The back door's lock had been blown off and the door was half-open.

"I thought you said Axel shot trespassers," said Eddie, looking at Knox.

"Seems like he did," said Julianna, pointing with her gun at the body lying just inside the doorway. She stepped around them and kicked open the door all the way. Another Kezzin lay farther inside.

"A-axel…" Knox stammered and tore around Julianna straight into the second floor. She reached out for him but dropped her hand, giving up before she'd even tried.

Eddie launched forward to stop Knox, but Julianna held up a hand to halt him. Knox was already in the main room of a loft building.

"It's too late," she said in a whisper.

Eddie mouthed, "What?" and narrowed his eyes, gazing down the narrow hallway that led into darkness. It took several moments for his eyes to adjust and the figure sprawled on the ground to come into focus. Knox had knelt and was shaking the body, rocking its shoulders.

"Do you suppose?" asked Eddie, letting the question hang quietly in the air.

Julianna slowly nodded and her eyes slid to the side vacantly, indicating she was speaking with Pip.

A moment later she straightened, looking tense. "We've got company. There're Brotherhood ships in orbit, and they appear to be waiting for us."

Eddie nodded. He didn't like what he was going to have to do next, but it couldn't be helped. "Gunner, we've got to go."

Knox looked up, eyes wide. He seemed to have forgotten where he was. After a long few seconds he pushed to his feet and walked to where Eddie was waiting.

"We've got company," said Eddie. "We need to get back to the ship."

Knox wasn't shaking, but Eddie was certain the boy was rattled. Before they continued, Eddie placed his hand on his new friend's shoulder. "I'm sorry we didn't make it in time."

"I am too," muttered Knox, "but at least he didn't suffer, right? Or is that just something people say to make themselves feel better?"

Eddie didn't know what to tell him. Knox had lost so much, time and time again. He pointed to the stairs, suggesting that Knox go out behind Julianna.

Without another word Knox complied, and Eddie quickly followed.

A hot wind blew hard, knocking sand into their faces, and Julianna put her arm over her face to shield her nose and mouth. She waited until the two had caught up with her.

"Protect your face. Looks like a dust storm is starting," she ordered.

Knox, using his good arm, pulled the bandana he'd been wearing around his neck up to just cover his nose. Julianna's eyes shot to the rag tied to Knox's arm and she realized Eddie didn't have his bandana anymore. It was only a thin piece of cloth, so one wouldn't think it would be that important, but in a dust storm it might be the difference between breathing and suffocating. She yanked her bandana off her neck and thrust it at Eddie. He looked up, bemused.

"No, I'm good," said Eddie, pulling his cowboy hat down over his eyes.

"You're only human. Take it." She refused to accept the bandana back. "I'm going to speed off and get the ship ready. Be prepared to jump in and take off when you get there."

Reluctantly Eddie consented, covering his mouth and nose with the cloth. The wind had kicked up, making visibility poor. Julianna gave them one last look before she streaked off, losing them at once as she headed farther into the storm.

"What did she mean by 'you're only human?'" asked Knox as he marched against the wind. It was impossible for them to sprint as Julianna had. They were striding straight into forty-mile-an-hour wind, and the dirt it threw up made it feel like they were walking into sandpaper.

Eddie only shook his head at the question, unwilling to speak as the dust storm continued to pick up. Knox asked a lot of questions, and he figured there would be many more. There had to be, because Eddie wasn't getting rid of Knox, not after he hadn't hesitated to save his life. Some people were taught to be good, and then there were those who were born that way. As far as Eddie could tell, Knox was definitely the latter.

Living outside of Federation space had kept Knox from knowing much about the civilization or culture of the bulk of humanity. He knew about ships and guns, but his concept of technology would be minimal. That was what happened when one wasn't raised in Federation space. He'd understand in time, but for now Eddie would ease him into it.

Visibility was so poor that part of Knox's face was

obscured, and before long they'd need to take shelter. Now Eddie understood what Hatch had meant about the weather in Gun Barrel. This place was meant for cowboys, who were tough enough to survive it.

Eddie grabbed Knox by the arm and pulled him close to the nearest building, under the porch eaves. It provided a bit of relief but not quite enough so he pushed forward again. He felt as though they were making no progress at all. They weren't even halfway down the main road, and the storm was still growing in ferocity. Was Julianna back at the ship? It was smart that she had returned, but what if they couldn't make it in time?

Knox, beside Eddie, was holding onto the side of the building and looked like he might blow away at any moment. Eddie could relate. He stomped forward, clapping his boots down but making no audible noise over the howling wind. He pulled his other boot to meet it, feeling as though he were walking through quicksand. Again he picked his foot up to step forward, but he was blown backward several inches instead. He got low to the ground to try a different tack, hoping to make progress.

Knox had been knocked off his feet, too. His face was covered in sand, and his eyes were like little green beams peering through the brown covering.

"Don't give up!" Eddie bellowed, crawling next to Knox on the wooden boards of the walkway. "We can do this!" The bandana flipped up, caught by the wind, and before Eddie could secure back on his face a mound of sand zoomed down his throat, instantly making him gag. He tried to breathe, and realized his nose was nearly stopped up from the harsh sand. They couldn't make it any farther.

Beside him Knox nodded. "We can do this," he said repeating Eddie's words but more softly.

The wind sounded like a shrieking siren and they could hardly make out the next few feet, but beside them was a door. All Eddie had to do was bust through it and they'd have the shelter from the harsh storm, but he looked toward the ship.

They couldn't desert Julianna. She'd wonder where they were, and if they had made it into a building. He tried to move forward once more and again was pushed back by the wind, and his gaze returned to the door. If they didn't get to shelter, they were going to die. Julianna would understand, and she'd find them once the storm passed.

Eddie tried twice to stand, but the wind battered him back down each time. Finally he threw all his weight into the effort and ran at the door, but it didn't budge. It had been reinforced—that was clear—probably to better withstand the storms. It would take more strength than he had remaining to bust through it. He pulled his body back to throw it into the door again. He had to try...

"Captain!" Knox yelled from behind him, sounding like he was far away despite only a few short meters' gap between him.

Eddie turned, shielding his eyes. Knox had hunched over, but he was pointing at something. Blinking, Eddie tried to understand what Knox was motioning to, but the storm was thick, offering them only brief moments of visibility.

Then, through the blinding wall of brown, Eddie saw a color. Blue at first, but then white. Light glistening, reflecting off something...

Something in the air.

The Q-Ship came toward them out of the cloud of sand and hovered over the main road only two meters from the walkway.

Eddie ran in that direction, grabbing Knox as he did and pulling him into the Q-Ship through the open hatch. Julianna had already retreated to the pilot's seat.

Once the two men had made it inside the door closed automatically behind them, sealing them away from the storm. Julianna glanced over her shoulder at Eddie and Knox. "Sorry I took so long," she told the two of them.

"Just in time," Eddie wheezed.

The Q-Ship rose higher as Eddie and Knox coughed and sputtered on the floor, and Julianna whipped her head over her shoulder. The two were coated in a thick layer of grit, as if they'd been dipped in oil and then a vat of sand.

Those guys were nearly goners. Fucking dust storm, Julianna said to Pip.

You'd be pretty sad if something happened to the Captain.

Don't tell me about sad, Pip.

I know what sadness feels like.

Let's save the existential talk for later.

Julianna sped the Q-Ship through the atmosphere and out into orbit.

Monitoring for Brotherhood vessels. There were two before, but they've changed locations.

Yes, why don't you do your job and stop making false observations?

You don't like me as much since I evolved to an AI, do you?

What did I say about dumb observations?

That you like them? teased Pip.

Eddie was now spitting clumps of dirt onto the floor. He was going to be no help for a bit longer.

I need you on the guns.

Need? I like it when you say that word. It makes you seem—

Like I'm not going to kick your ass?

That wasn't exactly what I was going to say. By the way, you've got two *Brotherhood ships cruising your way.*

So do you, so fire away.

Julianna spotted the approaching ships and jerked the controls to the side, spinning the Q-Ship in a half-circle. They nearly collided with one of the ships, but that offered more angles for Pip to fire. Three shots connected, but only caused surface damage.

Eddie and Knox had rolled during Julianna's acrobatics and were currently knocking around in the cargo area.

"Teach, get the two of you strapped in already. This ride is only going to get bumpier," said Julianna.

"Sure thing," wheezed Eddie. "We're just back here dying."

"Stop being so dramatic." Julianna now had both ships on her ass firing at her. She jerked to one side and then feinted, swerving farther the same direction. Flying the Omega was about like walking, just as natural and easy. The controls were intuitive. Hatch had built the perfect ship so far as Julianna was concerned, and she'd use it to kill every Brotherhood soldier she could find.

Once they were a good distance from the enemy she twisted the ship to the side, turning it around. Pip fired a bunch of rounds, many grazing the other ships but again not taking them out.

Fuck, Pip, where did you learn to shoot?

I think what you're saying is that you'd prefer the Captain to be in the copilot's seat, teased Pip.

That's not at all what I said. Your understanding of language is horrible. Get an education!

Eddie slammed into the chair next to Julianna. Over her shoulder she spied a strapped-in Knox, although he was still coughing wildly.

Eddie looked at her with his face still caked in dirt. "Ready to kick some Brotherhood ass?"

"I thought you'd never come to the party."

"Oh, am I off the guns then?" asked Pip from overhead, feigning annoyance. "I'll just go take a nap."

A missile hit the side of the ship and knocked them all forward from the blunt force.

"Why don't you keep an eye on enemy fire, Pip," yelled Julianna.

"Right, I can do that. Fire headed for port side," Pip informed her.

Julianna put the ship on its side to avoid the worst of the attack, then activated the thrusters and barreled between the two Brotherhood ships.

Eddie rolled out a spray of bullets, hitting one of the vessels' wings and sending it spiraling out of control toward the planet's surface.

"He's gonna feel that shit in the morning," said Eddie. He tried to laugh, only to wind up coughing.

"Yeah, and apparently that pissed off his buddy," she said, looking at Eddie.

She angled the ship so that the guns in the back were directed at the Brotherhood ship.

Eddie grabbed the weapons controls again and focused on targeting the incoming ship. When the vessel crossed their stern just as anticipated, Eddie punched the trigger and loosed a number of rounds at the small flyer, and multiple direct hits forced the little ship to fall back at once.

"Whew! *That's* what I'm talking about," said Eddie, his voice still scratchy from the sand.

A red light blinked on. "No partying just yet," said Julianna. "We've still got a problem."

9

Omega-line Q-Ship, Behemoth System

"If you're gonna tell me you left something in that piece-of-shit town, forget it. I'll buy you a new...whatever it is that you lost," said Eddie, trying to wipe sand from his face without getting it in his eyes. He needed a shower. A beer too. Actually, scratch the shower—he'd rather just have the beer.

"No, it's the ship," said Julianna, peering at the controls and gauges.

Eddie's vision, blurred by sand and whatever else the storm had thrown at him, couldn't make out much at a distance but he squinted, trying to determine what she was staring at that was a problem.

"It's the fuel lines," said Knox from the back.

Julianna turned around, surprised. "Yeah, it is. How'd you know that?"

"The fucking *fuel* lines? What's wrong with them?" asked Eddie.

"I'm guessing one of those attacks severed them somehow," Julianna said, still looking at Knox. "How'd you know?"

He shrugged. "I can feel the lag in the ship. The way it's doing it reminds me of when I have a blockage in one of my lines. The ship is getting fuel, but something is blocking it. Maybe the hose is bent from external damage on the ship."

Slowly Julianna turned and looked at Eddie with a strange expression on her face. "He knows mechanics?"

"Yeah, think we should hook him up with Hatch?" asked Eddie. They needed pilots, but that was a short-term goal. Mechanics were gold, especially for a covert operation like theirs. Thing was, the two roles usually didn't cross like they did in Knox—not unless it was someone like Hatch, but that octopus was an exception to every rule. Most people specialized in only one occupation, at least in the military. It seemed that out here, where staying alive relied on one's ability to diversify, people had no other choice but to become Jacks of All Trades.

"First things first," continued Julianna. "We need to find a place to land so we can fix the fuel line. There's no way we can make it back to *ArchAngel*, even if we jump."

"Jumping would be unadvisable under the current circumstances," said Pip from overhead.

"Whoa, who is that?" asked Knox, scanning the ship's ceiling.

Eddie laughed and kept watching the radar. "Meet Pip, our AI. He shares headspace with Julianna. Luckily for you, our buddy Hatch managed to interface the ship so Pip could talk out loud."

"Hello, Knox Gunnerson. It's a pleasure to meet you," said Pip.

"Uh. Hey. Thanks. Same, I guess," said Knox, his chin tilted at the ceiling.

"How's your arm?" Eddie asked him.

Knox looked down at the place where the bullet had gone through his arm. "It's fine. I actually forgot about it."

"We will get you stitched up when we get back to *Arch-Angel*," said Julianna.

Eddie stabbed his finger at a nearby planet on the radar. "That's where we need to land."

"Sagano?" asked Julianna. "Why there? I've got at least three other planets in closer range."

"Because there's a killer bar," said Eddie.

Julianna rolled her eyes but continued to fly the ship steadily. "Of course."

"The other planets are deemed mostly safe," Pip informed them.

"But they don't have a known place to get some R and R." Eddie looked at Julianna with his best puppy-dog face. "Need a place to wash off all this sand before I crack, and I promise—only one beer. Nothing crazy.'"

Julianna considered him for a moment before finally conceding. "Fine. You get your way, just this once."

"Are you kidding me?" asked Julianna, trying to open the door against the vines that had fallen on them when they landed. "This is a fucking jungle planet. What were you thinking, bringing us here?"

"Yeah, about that... Might have forgotten to mention most of the planet is undeveloped," said Eddie, scratching his head.

Julianna threw her shoulder into the hatch door, and branches broke behind it. She pushed it all the way down as vines snagged on the corners, mouth gaping.

"Teach, is this your idea of a practical joke?" asked Julianna, staring out at the dense jungle covered in moss and teeming with plants. Trees grew on top of trees like they'd run out of space and were playing 'King of the Mountain.'

From the air Julianna had noticed the area being heavily covered in forest, but she'd had no idea it was this overgrown. The vegetation looked completely different from the ground. She even landed on a small platform, but it seemed no one had cleared the vines to prevent them from hanging over and obstructing it.

Eddie scoffed. "Oh, come on. If I was going to play a practical joke it would be way better." He peered out of the ship, squinting against the greenish light filtering in from overhead. "We're just a bit off the path. I was all turned around before, but I know where the bar is from here."

How Eddie could understand where he was going when the jungle looked the same from every angle was beyond her. "What about the ship? Broken fuel lines, remember?" said Julianna, throwing her hand up.

"We'll hit up Hatch when we get back here and see if he can talk us through the fix, but first this cowboy needs to clean up. There's sand covering all my parts, if you know what I mean," said Eddie, walking forward stiffly. "Come on, Knox, I'll buy you a round."

Knox, who was as crusty as Eddie, looked at Julianna tentatively as he passed.

Julianna had Pip cloak the ship as she disembarked. Above her head birds flew through the trees, chirping loudly. It had been a long time since she had been in a jungle, and the scent of the greenery brought back memories of early missions when she was younger and the job was still new to her.

After a few paces she noticed that her feet felt lighter, her chest swelled more fully, and the moist forest air had become easier to breathe. Maybe taking the detour to Sagano hadn't been such a bad idea after all.

———

"Oh, look who the cat dragged in!" a burly man boomed as soon as Eddie had pushed through the swinging doors into the bar. The building didn't really have walls. It was mostly surrounded by mesh curtains attached to its thatched roof. Bamboo poles supported the structure, and the floor was covered in handwoven mats and dirt from outside, making it feel as though it were part of the jungle.

Knox froze just beside Eddie, fists clenched at his sides, and behind them Julianna stared at the dozen locals gathered around the tiki bar.

The thick-chested man thrust out of his seat, making it fall back on the floor, and the three men at his table looked up with sneers on their dirty faces. They all had black hair and tanned skin, and their eyes were bloodshot from too many servings of Sagano moonshine—or Brick Walls, as the locals called it.

"Hey, you!" yelled the man in Eddie's direction.

"Hey, you withered piece of dung!" Eddie yelled back. He straightened and took in the many faces that turned to look at him. Julianna stepped in front of Knox, placing herself between the boy and these ruffians.

"I didn't think you'd ever show your face in here again!" As the man strode toward them it became clear that he was easily seven feet tall, and his chest was twice as wide as Eddie's.

"Me either. Didn't think I'd ever have the misfortune of seeing that disgusting, sorry excuse for a face ever again," said Eddie.

Julianna tensed next to him, her hand twitching inches from her gun.

A loud laugh boomed from the man as he halted in front of Eddie. Julianna started to push him away, but corrected herself when he only leaned forward and pulled the Captain in for a hug, their chests bumping.

"You old sonofabitch," bellowed the man, stepping back. "Where you been, Blackbeard?"

"Nowhere special," said Eddie, tipping his head to Julianna and Knox. "Meet Sabien, you two. He owns the Hole in the Jungle."

Julianna looked around. "I don't know, I wouldn't call it that. I like the open-air feel of it," she said, stepping forward and taking Sabien's hand. His eyes widened when Julianna shook it. He'd obviously tried another one of his strong-arm shakes, but he had underestimated the woman.

"No, the name of the bar is 'Hole in the Jungle,'" explained Eddie.

Sabien laughed. "Remember the last time you were in

here? It looked completely different then," he said, motioning to the room, which was sprinkled with stools and a few tables.

"Yeah, I like the new design," Eddie assured him.

Sabien looked at Julianna and Knox. "After the last time Blackbeard was here I had to have the entire place remodeled."

"This piece of shit needed it," said Eddie. "I just helped with the demolition, so you could fix things up."

Sabien chuckled, waving him off. "He destroyed the entire bar in less than a minute. It took me weeks to renovate after that."

"Those guys deserved it," said Eddie, watching as three men got up and left via the back entrance. There were still roughly ten people in the bar.

Sabien chuckled. "Friends of Eddie's are probably trouble, but what the hell? Saddle up to the bar. Drinks on the house for you two." Sabien motioned to Julianna and Knox. "I'd say the same for Blackbeard, but I'd have no stock left. I'll buy you *one* drink, old friend, but that's my limit."

Eddie smiled widely, looking at Julianna. "Appearances might be a little deceiving if you think I'm the one you've got to worry about. Right, Jules?"

Sabien dismissed this and marched toward the bar. "Two Brick Walls for these folks, and a Singapore Sling for the lady," he called to the bartender, who was a short man with shifty eyes, a round belly, and a flat nose. He was polishing glasses, but he nodded to the bar owner and went to work making the drinks.

"I'm not sure about a Brick Wall," said Eddie. "I've got to keep my wits about me. I have to fly later."

"You're flying again, Blackbeard? That's great," Sabien exclaimed. A few of the men at a table nearby looked up, their attention piqued. Sabien glanced out the nearby window. "Where's your ride?"

"We parked it over there," said Eddie, pointing in the opposite direction of where the Q-Ship was located. Julianna caught this and narrowed her eyes as she surveyed the bar. Eddie slammed an open palm on the bar. "I'll take a Blue Ale."

"All we've got are Douglas Adams here," the guy said.

Eddie nodded. "Fine, we'll take two of those, as long as they're cold."

"So, Blackbeard," Sabien said, "I have to know. Why do you look like absolute shit?"

Eddie ran his hand over his face and sand sprinkled away. He'd nearly forgotten he was still so filthy. "Oh, *that*. We got stuck in a storm. Think you can help us out?" He motioned to Knox and the bandage on his arm.

"Washroom is over there, same as before." Sabien pointed a finger toward a side area where the mesh curtains were parted.

"All right. Let's go, Knox," said Eddie. "The water in the basins is full of parasites, but I think I'd prefer that over getting *more* sand in my eyes. We'll just have to take an immune booster when we get home."

"I heard that!" barked Sabien.

The bartender slid a pink drink in a tall glass in front of

Julianna. It was garnished with something that looked like pineapple but had spikes on the skin.

"What's that?" asked Julianna, looking at Sabien and pointing at the frilly drink.

"That's a Singapore Sling, a classy drink for a classy little lady," he said, his tone different than when he spoke to Eddie. "Don't you worry, there's not too much liquor in there. You won't even taste it."

Julianna eyed the drink like it was a slimy Trid head on a stick.

"Go on there, honey, taste it. You'll like it. Real sweet. About like you, I'm sure," said Sabien.

Julianna's jaw clenched and she pushed the drink away. "Look, *honey*, I appreciate the drink, but if it's all the same I'll take one of those Brick Walls."

Sabien chuckled dismissively and leaned casually on the bar, making it groan from his weight. "That's funny. Those are too strong for you. We call them 'Brick Walls' for a reason, if you get me." He winked at her.

"I think you're one who doesn't understand. I'd like to try one of those." Julianna lifted her eyes and looked at the bartender, who was pretending to not listen to the exchange. "Thanks for this drink, but I can't drink anything pink. It will make me break out in hives. A Brick Wall instead."

The bartender looked at Sabien, who nodded reluctantly. "Give the lady what she wants." He turned to Julianna. "So how do you know Blackbeard?"

Julianna was aware that everyone in the bar was pretending to not listen to them. "We work together."

"Work together, eh? What kind of *work* is he doing

these days? Still beating up pirates and getting himself into trouble?" Sabien scratched his stubbled chin.

The bartender slid a tumbler half-filled with an amber liquid in front of Julianna. "Thanks," she said, not looking at the guy.

"Take it slow. Take a sniff of it, and if you can handle that you can try sipping the stuff," said Sabien, his voice cautious.

Julianna picked up the tumbler and slung the drink back. It ran down her throat, filling her insides with warmth. It didn't burn like she'd figured it would, but it coated her mouth and made her lips pucker.

"Whoa!" Sabien exclaimed as he straightened, his dark eyes wide. "You're gonna feel that, honey."

Julianna blinked and looked around the bar, not really affected by the shot. It had just made her fingers tingle. She slammed the tumbler on the bar. "I'll take a double this time."

Sabien shook his head, looking from the questioning bartender to Julianna. "I'm not sure that's a good idea."

"I thought you said it was all on the house for us? You're not going back on that now are you, *darling*?" asked Julianna. The guys at the table weren't even making a show of not paying attention now, and the ones at the bar kept looking at the exits. *For fuck's sake, Teach had known what he was doing coming to this bar*, she thought. He had been looking for a drink and a bit of something else.

The bartender complied, filling her glass. "Leave the bottle," she ordered, and the bottle hovered over the surface of the bar for a moment before he set it all the way down.

Eddie and Knox returned just as Julianna took a long sip of the drink, not throwing it back like the first. Both guys' hair was still dripping wet, like they'd submerged their heads in buckets of water. Knox's Mohawk was slicked back, and about the same color as Eddie's dark hair.

"I feel better," said Eddie, taking the freshly opened bottle of beer and sitting on the bar.

Sabien was still regarding Julianna like she was a new species. "Your lady—she's a bit different, ain't she?" he asked Eddie.

Julianna threw the drink back. She was a bit impatient that the liquor wasn't even giving her a buzz, so with a steady hand she picked up the bottle and poured another.

"She's not my lady, and you might want to watch how you talk about her if you value your life," said Eddie, taking a sip of his beer.

Sabien shook his head of greasy black hair like he was trying to shake away a strange thought. "I don't know how you do it, Blackbeard. You're always—"

A loud bang erupted from the other side of the bar, and Julianna lazily looked up. A man about as big as Sabien had just pushed through the swinging doors, making them crack against the support posts.

"Blackbeard..." the man growled, chin low and black eyes smoldering. "How dare you return!"

Eddie rolled his eyes like he'd just encountered a mild inconvenience. "I dared, if you can believe it."

"Cousin, I told you that you were only welcome here if you didn't cause trouble." Sabien stepped forward.

Cousin? Julianna examined the two giant men, suddenly noticing their resemblance to one another even though it wasn't easy to spot. The one who had just entered was a great deal uglier, and had deep wrinkles around his mouth and eyes like he'd spent far too long in the sun.

The man looked past Sabien and pinned his eyes on Eddie. "And I told *you*, Sabien, I'd be okay as long as that maggot didn't show back up." Behind the man were the guys who had fled the bar earlier, their faces angry now.

Eddie took a long drink of his beer before slamming it onto the bar, and unhurriedly looked at the man. "Ink, are you still beating up on poor souls who land on Sagano and taking half of their supplies as 'tax?'" There was a new heat in Eddie's voice—a vengeance Julianna had seen before. It reminded her of the first time she'd met him back in the Five Trees Bar.

"What me and my boys do is none of your business. I think I told you that before," said Ink, balling up one of his fists and punching the massive palm of his other hand.

"And I thought I taught you a lesson last time." Eddie approached the other man but Sabien was still between them, looking at each and trying to decide what to do.

"You taught me *nothing*. A guy's got to make a living, and that's all we're doing," said Ink.

"By pillaging the innocent? Why don't you try getting a job like your cousin?" asked Eddie, shaking his head at the brute.

Julianna took a casual sip of her drink and let her eyes drift to Knox, who was scanning the bar. If he was paying attention to the nonverbal cues, then he knew that half the bar were Ink's supporters. The rest just wanted to get drunk and had no horse in this race. The bartender, though...he was the fucking problem, Julianna observed, watching the round man continue to polish glasses and pretend not to notice the growing disturbance.

Ink cracked his knuckles in the palm of his other hand and laughed, pasting a wide sneer on his face. "You still not okay with the Saganoans taking what belongs to us?"

"I'm not okay with you bullying everyone who lands here," said Eddie.

"I've got to make a living," said Ink.

"Sell a fucking product, like liquor." Eddie jerked a thumb in Sabien's direction. He'd backed off, mouth pursed and head shaking at his cousin.

"Ink, you know how I feel about what you do," said Sabien.

"So you're just going to sit by once again while I teach this maggot-breath a lesson?" asked Ink.

"I believe it was your head that I stuck through the bar the last time," said Eddie, indicating the new and still-pristine bar.

"Well, things will be different this time." The two men beside Ink stepped up, each pulling a long stick from behind his back. They were essentially batons, but had been painted black and had nails hammered through them, making them sharper and harder in places.

Julianna still hadn't risen from her place at the bar, and now she picked up the bottle and poured another glass. Knox was vibrating with nerves, she observed. She caught his attention and as she brought the glass to her lips she mouthed the words, "No guns."

His anxious eyes widened, but he gave a minute nod.

"Sorry, Cousin, but unless you kick these scum out I'm going to have to tear up the bar again," said Ink to Sabien.

After a tentative glance at Teach, Sabien shook his head. "It's me who is sorry, Cousin. We might be blood, but Blackbeard is right. I'd rather have no bar then condone what you do." He cast a look at Teach, his eyes disappointed. "Do what you gotta do."

The two men flanking Ink smacked the batons into their palms, making a slapping sound.

"Oh look, Smelly and Smellier have decided to join the fight." Eddie leaned to the side, his voice directed to the bartender. "Can my friend and I get another round? We're about to be thirsty."

The first man stepped forward and swung his baton, which made Eddie arch his back as he retreated a few steps to keep his midsection from getting nailed. Knox bolted from his position and went after the other man, who was trying to double-up on Eddie.

As Ink watched this he laughed loudly, as if he'd already won the fight.

Within seconds Eddie had the first man in a head-lock, his face red from lack of oxygen. He dropped his baton as a few men bolted out of the bar, but the others joined the fight.

Knox ducked several times, not hitting his opponent but not getting hit either.

Julianna took a sip of her drink, watching the scene with mild interest.

The first man was out cold, and Eddie picked up a chair and took out three more with a single swing. Several others charged him as though their numbers would somehow balance the scales, but Eddie was made for this. As the scene intensified and the battle continued, his eyes grew hard and his mind clear. He was in his element, acting on sheer instinct.

The grin had disappeared from Ink's face by this time, replaced by a drooping scowl as his concern grew.

When the man with the baton swung hard at Knox, he slid to the ground and kicked his legs out from under him. The man landed hard on his back and Knox knocked the baton to the other end of the bar. With another swipe of his leg Knox buried his foot in his opponent's temple, knocking him out.

Now there were only three remaining—Ink and two of his cronies. That was when Julianna noticed that the bartender had set his dirty rag on the bar and was scratching his forehead. Then he lowered his hand and pretended to feel around his apron.

But Julianna was no fool.

When the bartender brought the hidden pistol out from under his belt, Julianna picked up the bottle of Brick Walls and threw it past him to crash into the shelf behind him. He flinched and shot her a look.

She stared at him steadily, breathing calmly with no fear or concern in her eyes. "Get the fuck out of here," she told him, "before the next one hits your head.

The bartender looked down at his gun and then at Julianna, unable to hide his worry. Julianna could sense him holding his breath.

The second he breathed again he dashed to the side, and his gun fell to the floor where he had been standing. Julianna watched him flee through the swinging doors at the front of the bar. She couldn't blame him for being a coward, not in this instance. Not against her.

The commotion on the other side of the bar had grown now that Eddie battled Ink. Knox had taken on the last two men. Julianna threw the rest of her drink back before lazily standing and stretching her arms. She ambled over to where Ink had Eddie pinned against a support post. The brute's head was pressed hard into Eddie's abdomen, and the post was groaning from the force.

"Hey there, Jules!" exclaimed Eddie, grimacing from the pressure.

"How's it going, Teach? Need some help?" asked Julianna. In the background, Knox had finished off the remaining two goons.

"If you're not busy," wheezed Eddie, giving her a grin.

Julianna poked Ink on the shoulder and he stood up, but he still didn't let Eddie go. "What do you...want, woman?" the giant wheezed.

"I was hoping to get into the fight," said Julianna. "You'll need to let him go first, though."

The large man regarded Julianna for a moment and then howled with laughter. "Sure thing, sweetheart. Let me just put his head through the bar. It's only fair."

"I'm afraid I need his head intact," she said, frowning. "You have three seconds to step away from him." She planted her weight on her back foot.

Ink laughed a second time and, turning back to the Captain, squeezed Eddie with both arms.

Julianna sighed and shook her head. "Have it your way," she said, then launched up and forward, sending her hand straight down into the man's neck. The giant's head rebounded, and he released Eddie and staggered back from the attack.

Eddie stepped forward and lifted his fist into Ink's chin, smashing his lip and spilling his blood.

The man spun and faced Julianna, and she grinned up at him. "Hello there, sweetheart," she said as she sent a knee straight into his belly and then a foot into his groin.

He doubled over and collapsed, struggling to breathe as his eyes rolled back in pain. "B-bastards..." Ink muttered before passing out.

Eddie looked around the bar, finally noticing the mess he'd made. "Oh, shit!"

Sabien stood on the far side of the bar with a beer still in his hand.

"Sorry about the place, old buddy," Eddie said, scratching his head.

Sabien stared at his unconscious cousin and the other men who were scattered on the floor around the bar and shook his head. "Don't be. Hopefully they've learned their lesson this time."

Julianna's eyes fell on Ink, who was lying at her feet. "Maybe," she said, bending down beside him, "but some people never change."

"Anyone can change," said Eddie, who walked up to her and gave her a warm smile. "But it takes some people a little more time than others."

Planet Sagano, Behemoth System

The jungle was growing darker, and there were strange animals scurrying through the trees. Reflective eyes popped up in the dark canopy as the three made their way back to the ship.

Julianna pushed through the large leaves and low-hanging vines. "Next time, do you think you could give me a heads-up that you're taking us to a place where someone wants you dead?"

Eddie pretended to consider this, then shook his head. "It's more fun this way. You should just go ahead and assume they want me dead in most places."

Knox hadn't said a word since they left the Hole in the Jungle, but he'd kept his eyes on Julianna and his mouth parted most of the way like he wanted to say something. Finally he strode up next to her, although it was hard to walk shoulder to shoulder on the narrow jungle path. "You aren't normal, are you?"

A laugh burst from Eddie's mouth. He couldn't help it. So many things were new to Knox, and watching him learn about the strange and awesome stuff the Federation had and did was like seeing it for the first time again himself.

Julianna didn't laugh, but instead pursed her lips. "What's 'normal?'"

"Right, good question. I just meant that you're different, like not human," said Knox, his voice hesitant.

Again Eddie laughed, thoroughly amused. "She's an alien."

"I'm enhanced," she corrected. "I'm still human, but my nanotechnology makes me stronger and faster, and I have regenerative abilities."

"Ask her how old she is!" Eddie urged.

"That's rude, Teach," said Julianna, pretending to be offended.

"I'm guessing you're old. Are you the least bit drunk from that Brick Wall stuff?" asked Knox.

Julianna tilted her head back and forth as if weighing her answer. "I'm a bit more relaxed, but I wish I hadn't smashed that bottle. I could have used one more drink."

"That's what *I* do to her. I drive her to drink more," said Eddie, proudly.

"Damn, you already had a few shots of that stuff," said Knox.

They'd arrived back at the Q-Ship, and it uncloaked itself.

"Pip hasn't had any luck getting ahold of Hatch, so we might have to wait it out here until we can connect," Julianna informed them.

Eddie drew in a breath and pushed his back into a

nearby tree, leaning his weight into it. "That's fine with me. I could use a nap after all that fun."

Knox squatted down at the back of the Q-Ship, feeling around for the seam where the fuel lines were located. "I can see if I can find where the hose is pinched." He looked over his shoulder at the others, his face unsure. "I mean, if that's all right? I don't know much, and nothing about this ship, but I got a thing for mechanics."

Eddie shrugged, closing his eyes for a moment. "Totally fine with me."

"I'll grab you some tools." Julianna opened the hatch and climbed into the ship. "Pip says he might be able to talk you through some troubleshooting techniques," she yelled to Knox from inside.

Landing Bay, QBS *ArchAngel*, Behemoth System

Hatch was in the middle of yelling at three crew members when the Q-Ship landed aboard the *ArchAngel*. His tentacles waved wildly over his head, and his face was scrunched with frustration. The Londil brought his gaze to the vessel as the three disembarked, eyes narrowing on each of them before focusing on the ship itself.

"Sir, will that be all?" asked one of his mechanics.

Hatch turned back to the man. "Now you listen to me," he snapped. "Try that procedure again and this time don't screw it up, you good-for-nothing knuckle-dragger! That goes for the lot of you!"

The three crew members stiffened at the order, no doubt terrified.

Hatch looked back at the Q-Ship and puffed his cheeks,

then waddled over to Julianna and Eddie. "I got a message that you'd had an accident and needed my help. What are you doing back? I was just about to leave to pick you up."

"The Brotherhood ships hit us as we were leaving," said Eddie. "Luckily, old Knox here managed to get the busted fuel line fixed all by himself." He slapped Knox on the back. "He did it before I even managed to fall asleep, and you know how I like my naps." Eddie yawned loudly.

Hatch studied the boy before him with a cynical expression on his face. "You? *You* fixed the Q-Ship?"

Knox stared back at him timidly. "I, uh…"

"What's wrong?" asked Eddie, tilting his head. "You've never seen an octopus alien mechanic before?"

"This is Knox Gunnerson," said Julianna. "Knox, meet Hatch. He's a Londil, and our resident specialist in all things mechanical, electronic, and so on."

Eddie nodded. "Need a device, go to Hatch. Need a part, go to Hatch. Need—"

Hatch cut Eddie off. "Need a pain in the ass, go to the Captain."

"It's true, I'm a huge pain. Just ask Jules," said Eddie, jerking a thumb in her direction.

Hatch looked at Knox. "Pip said there was a problem with the fuel lines. Did you patch a leak? I guess that's easy enough to handle."

"Actually, the second interior armor plate had shifted and pinched the lines. I hammered it back into place and that fixed the issue," said Knox, shrugging noncommittally. "It wasn't really difficult."

"No, it doesn't sound like it," agreed Hatch, and turned back to look at his crew. "But the dimwits around *here* wouldn't have figured it out!" He raised his voice to make sure they could hear him. "They can't tie their *damn shoes*, let alone follow the specs for building a Q-Ship!" Hatch looked at Julianna and Eddie again. "Hope you don't need new ships anytime soon, because these monkeys can't seem to build one."

"We'll need more sooner rather than later," said Julianna. "Maybe Knox could help?"

Eddie tapped his chin. "We need good pilots, though, and he can handle himself in the air, can't he?"

Hatch looked between the two with an annoyed expression on his face. "And heaven forbid you ask the kid what *he* wants."

Knox shook his head, face slightly pink. "It's fine. I'll do whatever you need. I mean, *if* you're going to let me stay and...work with you, or whatever you have in mind."

Julianna looked at Eddie, and the two had a silent exchange. After a moment she nodded. "Knox, after seeing what you did back there in both Gun Barrel and Sagano, you've proven yourself to be an asset."

"An asset?" he asked.

"That means she likes you," said Eddie. "Would you like to join our team, fighting bad guys and protecting the Federation?"

Knox looked at the three of them like he expected someone else to answer for him.

Eddie continued, "It's your call, Knox. You saved my life back there in the desert, and in my book that means you've proven yourself a dozen times over." He motioned at the spot on the boy's arm where he'd been shot. "What we do is dangerous. I think you understand that now, but just in case you don't, take a listen and mind what I say. The people we fight are *scoundrels*, cold-blooded fiends with a thirst for killin'. They've drawn a line and dared the rest of the galaxy—namely us—to cross it." He looked at Julianna and Hatch, then at Knox again. "It's tough, doing what we do. Not a lot of people can."

"Which is why we're here," added Julianna. "Because we have the capability to cross that line and hold our ground."

Eddie nodded, and he gave the boy a wicked grin. "Plus, it's a hell of a lot of fun."

"Would our missions be like Sagano?" asked Knox.

"Well, bar fights aren't really in the job description," said Julianna. "They're more of an extracurricular activity."

Knox was quiet for a moment, as if he were weighing the variables in his head.

"Why don't you think on it for today?" asked Eddie. "You can decide if you want to join after we've gotten that wound looked at and had some rest. Take some time and watch what we do. Hang around *ArchAngel*, and when you're ready let us know."

Knox smiled, shaking his head. "No, I definitely want to join. Definitely," he said quickly. "I just don't know what I want to *do*. I like to fly, but mechanics comes naturally for me."

"Good," said Eddie. "Think about that decision instead, then. It's equally important."

Hatch motioned with his tentacle. "Well, now that you humans are done with your moment, get out of my landing bay! I've got work to do." He waddled past them and over to the Q-Ship, starting to inspect it at once.

Julianna smirked as she watched the octopus, then

turned to Eddie. "Pip has decoded the information he downloaded from Gun Barrel, by the way. He's sending it to Jack now. We should head to his office and review it together. Think you can hold off on that nap for a while?"

Eddie frowned. "Aw, fine. I guess stopping a galactic threat is more important than sleeping." He waved at Knox as he and Julianna strode to the exit. "Go explore the ship, kid, but don't do anything I wouldn't do!"

"You like Gunner," said Eddie, his tone teasing.

Julianna cast a sideways look at him, not at all impressed. "I think he has a good heart."

"But you're not as cautious about him as you were before, are you?"

The two walked through the corridor, crew members nodding in respect to them as they passed them.

"I think things have changed. He can't really get himself in trouble on *ArchAngel*. We'll see how he does, but yes, giving him a chance made sense," said Julianna, then added, "I think we should still be careful."

"You're always careful."

"Is this when you tell me I should live a little?" asked Julianna.

The pair rounded the corner and walked straight into Jack's office. "Nah, this is when I tell you not to change. You're the careful one, and I'm—well, the free spirit."

Jack looked up from a report he was studying. "Captain, did you just describe yourself as a 'free spirit?'"

"Well, I'm not like those hippies who run the crystal

store on Onyx Station, but sure. I'm the relaxed one, and Jules is the careful one. It's a nice balance," said Eddie, taking a seat.

"Let's get right to it. Now then, thank you for getting this information to me quickly. I've just reviewed it." Jack pushed away from his desk, crossing his ankle over his knee. "Tell me, what did you learn in Gun Barrel?"

"That our contact had been murdered and the Brotherhood is one step ahead of us," said Eddie.

"Damn it. I feared that Felix would go back and take out the person who vouched for him to the Defiance Trading Company. He's not leaving any loose strings out there, or so he thinks," said Jack.

"'So he thinks?' What did the report tell us?" asked Julianna, leaning on the back of the chair.

"It appears that Axel Link took an interest in Felix after he was 'asked' to provide a reference. I'm guessing he knew the guy was up to something. The information Pip pulled from Link's place shows that he was tracking an army, which I believe to be the Brotherhood," said Jack.

"Why is that news to us? We know the Brotherhood are Felix's minions," said Eddie, leaning back in his seat and stretching.

"Every time we get a glimpse of the Brotherhood their numbers grow. From what I've learned, it looks like the Brotherhood army has doubled since you went after Vas," said Jack.

"*Doubled?*" asked Eddie, leaning forward. He remembered the sea of soldiers they'd encountered when they came face to face with Commander Lytes and General Vas.

There had been more than they could handle, and that had only been a couple weeks ago.

"Yes, which means Felix and Commander Lytes are recruiting faster than ever. The information from Axel doesn't specify where the army is being housed, only shows when they were on the move. Still, that gave us a good enough estimate of their numbers to guess that they've doubled," said Jack.

"So now Felix has a huge store of weapons and is quickly growing an army…" said Julianna, voice trailing off and her eyes staring at nothing as she thought.

"Yes, which suggest he's preparing for a war," stated Eddie.

"Exactly. We suspected this was coming, but I don't think we could have guessed that he'd make this much progress so fast," said Jack.

"Especially after we destroyed his weapons cache. I would have thought it would take him a while to recover," said Julianna.

"We know roughly the size of his army," said Jack, no doubt trying to change the tone of the meeting from doubtful to optimistic. "And thanks to Knox, we also know what kind of weapons he acquired from the Defiance Trading Company. In truth, we know a great deal more today than we did yesterday, and I expect tomorrow we will learn even more. Progress takes time, my friends, but it will continue so long as we do our jobs."

Julianna nodded in agreement and responded, "We need to know more about his ship technology. More importantly, we need to know what he's planning next."

ArchAngel flickered onto the screen behind Jack, interrupting the meeting. "Hello, all," she said.

"Hey, A," sang Eddie.

"Jack, the contact has arrived and is currently with Officer Sours," said ArchAngel.

"Perfect timing. Thank you," said Jack to the AI, and turned his attention back to Eddie and Julianna. "As you mentioned, we need to know what Felix is planning next so we can get one step ahead of him."

"You brought in a contact who can help," guessed Julianna.

"That's right," he said with a knowing smile. "Marilla recruited this contact, and I think he might be quite insightful. Go down to the Intelligence Center, and let me know afterwards what you learned. Dismissed."

11

Intelligence Center, QBS *ArchAngel*, Behemoth System

Eddie's hand dove straight for his pistol upon entering the Intelligence Center and silently he pulled the weapon out, but left it pointed at the ground. Julianna tensed beside him, staring at the same threat with uncertainty in her eyes.

A huge Trid stood just in front of them, his back facing them. His long arms were stretched over his head and he stomped angrily. He obstructed the view of Marilla and Chester on the other side of him.

A loud roar spilled from the Trid's mouth, one that vibrated the room, and Julianna pulled her gun from her holster, holding it at the ready.

There was a small laugh. "Then what did you do?" asked Marilla, her voice light.

"Uhhh, Officer Sours, what's going on?" asked Eddie.

The Trid turned around and backed up at the sight of the weapons Julianna and Eddie held. Marilla sprang from

97

her seat and covered the Trid protectively with her small body, although she made a horrible shield.

"What are you doing? Rex isn't an enemy," said Marilla, her voice urgent.

Eddie eyed the Trid, who looked like he might have just peed his pants. He was large, but had the demeanor of a scared mouse.

"*This* is your contact?" asked Eddie.

She nodded. "Yes, I met Rex when I was doing the archeological dig on Kai. He's a friend, and a fellow scientist."

Eddie lowered his weapon and cast a glance at Julianna. "Jack could have told us in advance."

Julianna put her pistol away, shaking her head. "I think he's probably having a good laugh right now. We were obviously set up."

"I know many Trid are viewed as hostile and unwilling to work with humans, but I'm different," said Rex. His voice was squeaky, also reminiscent of a mouse's.

Marilla let out a steadying breath, then stepped to the side. "Rex, Captain Teach and Commander Fregin. They're the ones you'll report to."

Rex nodded and took a seat in one of the chairs, but he didn't fit quite right due to his size and stood again. Eddie pictured him as a giant teddy bear. Well, one with gills. A sweet shark-bear. He didn't have the angry and predatory look on his face that all the other Trid seemed to wear.

Chester covered a grin when the giant Trid clumsily knocked over the chair while trying to lever himself out of it.

"You're not working for the Kai government anymore,

is that correct?" asked Julianna, also trying to keep her face impassive. Eddie, though, wasn't really hiding his amusement.

"That's right. I worked with the research organization with Marilla, but I've been out of government business for a while. The things the Kai government has been dabbling in were questionable, mostly because the people they were working with... Well, it didn't seem right to continue," explained Rex.

"Do you mean the Brotherhood and Felix Castile?" asked Eddie.

Rex nodded, his dark shark-eyes becoming quite serious at the mention of Felix's name. "I used to work for Commander Vas, but when he left I used that as my opportunity to get out of Kai operations. I'm hoping to go back into research through the universities."

"Left?" asked Eddie. "You mean after we blew him up?"

Rex flinched at the question. "Yes, I guess I do."

"Tell them what you told me about Commander Lytes," urged Marilla.

"Oh, right. Well, General Vas was popular with his soldiers, but he was not as powerful as Commander Lytes. He's the real force behind the Brotherhood," said Rex.

"Yes, we're aware of that. What we need to find out is where the Brotherhood is and what they are planning next," said Eddie.

"That's where Rex can help," said Marilla, giving Rex an encouraging look. "Go on. They need to know so they can intervene."

Rex swallowed, something bobbing in his throat. "Well, I don't know where the Brotherhood is based, but I do know that Commander Lytes is planning on taking over a planet on the fringe. They may already be there, putting their plans into action. That's supposed to be their new base of operations."

"What?" asked Julianna in disbelief. "An entire planet? That's huge. Where? What is the name?"

Rex shook his massive head. "That I didn't find out. I left before any of the information crossed my desk."

"Where exactly did you work?" asked Julianna.

"The underwater base on Kai. It's under the eastern equator," explained Rex.

"Remember I told you that's where their ships are constructed? The Stingrays?" said Marilla.

"Did you work in R&D?" asked Eddie.

Rex bluntly shook his head. "I'm a historian, about like Marilla. I worked in the facility, but mostly on the dry land where the dig was taking place."

"Are you telling us that information on what the Brotherhood is planning can be found in this underwater facility?" asked Julianna.

"Pistris Station," supplied Rex. "And yes. Plans and technology are all housed in that particular station. I know I'm betraying my people, but since they've partnered with the Brotherhood, I believe their interests aren't pure. The Brotherhood has been giving huge donations to the Trid government in exchange for our compliance." Rex shook his head, looking disturbed. "But money isn't everything. I hear about what they're doing, and I can't be a part of that anymore."

His voice was almost frantic, maybe even scared.

"Like the planet you mentioned?" asked Eddie.

The Trid nodded. "They took over the planet and enlarged their military forces. My department was all but cut, since it wasn't vital to the mission. Most others were too, if they didn't serve the ever-increasing war machine. All the Brotherhood cares about is expanding its influence and control. I don't know specifics, but I know this is the start of something big. The power and influence of the Trid and Brotherhood are growing."

"I think we all know who is behind this, manipulating and using the Trid and Brotherhood," said Eddie, looking at Julianna. She agreed with a nod.

"Can you get back into Pistris Station?" asked Julianna.

Rex backed up several feet, nearly ramming into Chester. He looked as though he'd just been scared half to death. "Oh, no, I can't go back there. I quit. What if they suspected something? They'd throw me into prison. I can't have that."

"Right," said Julianna, drawing out the word. "Can you help *us* get into that underwater base?"

"Now you're talking," said Eddie, his tone excited. Breaking into a secret underwater base sounded like exactly what they needed to do next.

"I guess I could. You might still get caught, but I'll tell you what I know," said Rex.

Eddie clapped his hands and rubbed them eagerly. "Perfect." He turned to address Marilla. "Have Rex convey everything he knows about Pistris Station to ArchAngel so Hatch can work on a way for us to get into this base. Chester, you think you can hack the security system for us, grant us access?"

Chester spun around in his seat with a wide grin on his

face. "I must be a mind reader, since that's what I've been doing since Rex mentioned Pistris Station. I'll have your clearance by the end of the day."

Eddie let out a loud whoop. "That's what I'm fucking talking about!"

Bridge, QBS *ArchAngel*, Tangki System

The *ArchAngel* gated to the Tangki system, arriving near Kai's orbit.

"ArchAngel, can I please get an update on that information you've been hunting down for me?" asked Eddie, standing next to Jack on the bridge.

"Do you mean the information on how to get rid of that stubborn rash?" asked ArchAngel, her face on the large screen in the front. Many of the crew members at their different stations laughed.

"Ha-ha," said Eddie. "No, and I don't believe I asked for any such information."

Jack stood nearby. "You're still going through with this?" he asked. "Aren't you concerned about backlash from Julianna?"

"I've thought about it. I think this is what she needs, and I think there could be some long-term benefits," said Eddie.

"If you say so," said Jack. "Personally I'm going to avoid that woman's ire. She seems just as likely to rip your throat out as kiss you."

"More the former than the latter," said Eddie, "but I'll take my chances!"

"If the two of you are finished," said Archangel, "I've

found the information you requested, Eddie. I'll send it to you right now, along with those special rash remedies."

"Wow, thanks. You're a doll," said Eddie, humorlessly. He pulled up his pad, tapping the screen. "Here it is. And our current location, the Tangki system, couldn't be any more perfect. It's like it was meant to be."

"Serendipity," supplied ArchAngel.

Eddie looked up, confused. "Huh?"

"'Serendipity.' You said it was meant to be. That's the word for it," she said.

"Thanks. I'll use your expensive word the next chance I get," said Eddie.

Jack read the information on the pad over Eddie's shoulder. "I agree that the locations line up pretty well. Are you going to contact him?"

"Yes, I'll set up a meeting for when we return from Kai," said Eddie.

"You know that Julianna will more likely punch you for meddling than thank you," warned Jack.

"Meddling in what?" asked Julianna, popping up behind Jack and Eddie and nearly making them jump. *Damn! She was so fucking quiet,* thought Eddie.

He pushed the power button on the top of the pad and shook his head.

"We weren't talking about you. We were talking about Lars. I'm meddling in his love life. Trying to recruit a nice Kezzin girl for the crew," lied Eddie.

Julianna tilted her head to the side, not buying this at all. "I heard my name."

"Because we thought you wouldn't like us meddling in the crew's love life," said Eddie, his ears growing hot.

"Well, of course I don't. That's highly unprofessional. Jack, I'm surprised you'd condone such a thing," said Julianna, her tone punishing.

Jack yanked up his wrist, eyeing his watch. "I have a meeting in my office that I'm late for."

ArchAngel appeared on the main screen again. "Actually, Jack, I show that your afternoon schedule is wide open."

"Uhhh, I didn't put this meeting on my calendar," stuttered Jack, hurrying off.

Slowly, Eddie turned and looked at ArchAngel's face. "You have been *exceptionally* helpful lately."

Cargo Bay 01 , QBS *ArchAngel,* Tangki System

Hatch wiped a rag over his head, muttering to himself.

"The crew seems to be giving you a headache," stated Pip. "I show that your stress levels are elevated."

Hatch blew out an exaggerated breath. "That's because they are all a bunch of worthless idiots who need me to hold their damn hands."

"You *do* have eight tentacles. You could hold a few hands," joked Pip.

Hatch deflated his cheeks and stood back to stare at his current project. It was a rather *special* type of ship, somewhat different from the rest he'd recently been working on.

Pip continued, "And my records indicate that each member of your assigned crew has sufficient education to do the work you require of them. On the surface, they should be more than qualified to collectively build the Omega-line of Q-Ships."

"Education isn't everything," muttered Hatch. "I have plenty of degrees and certifications, but they'd all be worthless if I didn't have *instinct*. These people have book knowledge but no heart." He lifted a nearby screwdriver with a tentacle and examined a small bend in the metal before placing it down. "They don't know how to *feel* their way around a machine."

"What do you mean?" asked Pip.

"Ships are more than parts, Pip. They are living, breathing organisms that must be respected. The people on my crew are the same as all the other idiots I've met, with only a few rare exceptions. Those fools don't see the truth inside the metal, so they can't touch the soul of the ship they're working on. They can't understand how to talk to it, bend it, make it better. They don't know how to imagine anything more than what they *see*."

"Is that what you're doing right now? Trying to imagine something more?" asked Pip.

"I'm trying to figure out if I like the paint job," stated Hatch. "Blue is a good color for this one, don't you think?"

"Mmmm..." said Pip, thinking. "I would like a red racing stripe down the center. Maybe two."

Hatch dismissed the AI with a wave of his tentacle. "No, we're trying to camouflage it, not have the damn thing stick out like a sore appendage."

"Thumb," said Pip.

"What?" asked Hatch, mostly distracted.

"The expression is 'a sore thumb,'" stated Pip.

"I know damn well how it goes, but I don't have thumbs so why would I use such a dumb word?" replied Hatch.

The outer door opened and Julianna and Eddie strode into the bay.

"I always enjoy our little heart-to-heart talks," said Pip in a playful tone.

"Heart-to-hearts," corrected Hatch. "I have three hearts, remember?"

"And nine stomachs and blue blood," added Pip.

Hatch polished the vehicle in front of him as Eddie and Julianna approached.

"You called?" asked Julianna, smiling when she saw the mechanic. "We got a message to come and see you."

Hatch puffed his cheeks at the sight of her. "I did. I got your request for something to help you gain entry to the underwater base on Kai. Unfortunately, I don't have the time to create something from scratch. That would take longer than you have. Instead, I pulled one of my previous research projects from the storage locker."

"Is that a submarine?!" asked Eddie, looking at the blue ship. It was shaped like a "U" and had a round glass bubble in the middle.

"It is," said Hatch. "If I'd had more time I would've created a more unique one for your mission, probably with cloaking technology and big enough for more than one person. Instead, I tweaked this ship and got it working as well as could be expected," explained Hatch, stepping back and admiring the submarine.

"Wait, this only holds one person?" asked Julianna. "But we both need to get into the base."

"I'm sorry, Julie. Adding more room would require a

complete overhaul of the ship," stated Hatch. "That would take several days at the least, even for me. Weeks, if I left it up to my sorry excuse for a crew."

Defeated, Julianna blew out a breath. "Okay. It's not ideal, since I'd prefer us to partner up, but I'll just go into Pistris Station alone and—"

"Hey, whoa, no way!" argued Eddie. "I call dibs on this one."

"You can't call dibs on a mission," explained Julianna. "Besides, I got dibs when I volunteered myself."

"That's not how 'dibs' works," said Eddie.

She fanned her hand at him. "You'll just get caught if you go. Better to let an expert handle this."

"Who said I was going to get caught?" Eddie put a hand on his chest, offended. "There's no one down there but scientists and a few lazy guards. I can handle that easily."

"I'm the obvious choice," declared Julianna, a definitive tone in her voice.

"I disagree. I vote we settle this using a tried-and-true method," said Eddie.

Julianna lowered her chin and gave him a heated look. "Don't you dare say what I think you're going to say."

"*Roshambo!* That's the *only* fair way," said Eddie.

"What's that?" asked Hatch, who was watching all this unfold from the side.

"An old Earth game," said Julianna, glaring at Eddie. "It's just another name for rock-paper-scissors."

"Oh, I've seen that," said Hatch, "but unfortunately I've never been able to play." He held up a tentacle. "No fingers."

Julianna sighed. "Fine. We'll do this your way, Teach,

but *when* I win I want you to back off and let me go. No questions."

"You got it," he said, holding up his fist.

She did the same.

Eddie looked at Hatch. "You're the referee, buddy. Don't let me down!"

"Fine," said Hatch, waddling closer to the two of them and puffing his cheeks. "This seems like fun."

"Let's do this!" exclaimed Eddie.

"On the count of three," said Hatch. "One, two…three!"

Julianna pushed her fist through the air, but kept it tight.

Eddie's hand flattened.

"Ha! Paper beats rock!" Eddie beamed. "I get to drive a submarine." He shot his fist in the air to celebrate his success.

Julianna shook her head, looking dejected. "Fine. You get to go, but you'd better not get yourself into any trouble."

"Come on, have a little faith, would you? When did I ever do that?" asked Eddie. He strode over to the submarine and peered into the bubble.

"Like I said, I didn't have a chance to put cloaking technology into this ship," said Hatch. "Just getting it ready took a while. However, I *did* have it painted blue, which should help a little, and of course there's special plating to avoid radar detection," said Hatch.

"It's great, Doc. Is it easy to drive?" asked Eddie.

"I think you'll manage. Also, I loaded an interface into it so Pip can speak with you." He puffed his cheeks. "You'll have Julie on the comm. I *would* say there's no way you could screw it up, but you'll probably wreck the submarine, if I know you."

"I like it when you say nice things to me, Hatch," grinned Eddie. "I'll do my best to bring it back in one piece." He ran his hand over the sleek body of the sub.

"Originally, when I was assigned this task," began Hatch, "I wanted to create something like the Stingrays the Trid have been using. However, creating duel engines for both space and underwater travel was difficult at the time, so I created this as a half-measure with plans to develop it further."

"I'm shocked. That's a first for you, isn't it?" asked Eddie.

Hatch pretended he hadn't heard him and turned to Julianna. "It would be most helpful if your space chimp could find plans for the Stingrays while he's searching the base. It would take me a few months to create one myself, so that would save me a great deal of time. There's only one of me."

Julianna nodded. "We'll see what we can do, Hatch. If Pip is close enough while interfaced in the submarine, maybe he can pull that information from the network."

"I had a similar idea," said Hatch. "I'm not sure about the security of the Trid network for Pistris Station. You'll want to speak with Chester about that, I'd imagine."

"Already done," said Julianna. "He's working on finding back doors so once we're in we can get you full access."

"Then it looks like you have everything you need to succeed." Hatch looked at Eddie. "Just make sure you bring me those plans."

Omega-line Q-Ship, Planet Kai, Tangki System

It was strange for Eddie not to be sitting beside Julianna in the Q-Ship. Marilla had taken his seat, since he'd have to rely on her to navigate him around Pistris Station. Rex had been more than helpful in providing a layout for the facility. However, there were many parts of the building that were unique to the Trid staff, so having Marilla on the comm would help if Eddie encountered something Rex had forgotten to mention.

"We're nearing the drop," said Julianna. "Get into place, Blackbeard." She was flying the Q-Ship over the shimmering blue waters of Kai, which was mostly covered by seas. The base was sealed off, though, due to the requirements of the facility. Water made certain tasks more difficult, particularly with weapons research and ship construction.

Eddie slid into the submarine, pulling the hatch closed

as he dropped in. He buckled it shut and a green light came on to show that it was sealed properly.

"Blackbeard, can you hear me?" asked Julianna over the comm.

"Copy, Strong Arm. I'm in position," he said. "This sub is cozy, about like the backseat of a Volkswagen."

"A quick comparison shows that the backseat of a Volkswagen has a few dozen more centimeters of leg room," stated Pip.

"I could use the extra space," admitted Eddie, adjusting his body.

"You want to change places with me?" said Julianna.

"Nice try, Strong Arm, but I don't think so," said Eddie, grinning. He got to drive a submarine into an alien facility. It felt like his birthday, without the cake and shot of Nipponese ouzo, which was a 200-proof spirit. He also wouldn't have a hangover tomorrow, so it actually wouldn't be like his birthday at all.

Too bad about that.

"I'll release you now," said Julianna. "We're just off the surface. You'll be dropped on my count."

"I'm ready," stated Eddie, grabbing the submarine's controls. It was very similar to flying a ship, for which he was glad. If he wrecked the submarine he'd never hear the end of it from Hatch.

"Disembarking in five, four, three, two…and one," said Julianna.

The submarine tilted to the side and slid down, gaining momentum until it splashed into the blue waters of Kai. Eddie turned on the engines, submerging the submarine before he could be seen. Because the Q-Ship was cloaked, there was no way anyone would see *it*. They'd also picked an off-hour when the base and the water space above it were mostly empty, according to Rex. It was also mid-afternoon, which Rex had said was when most Trid took their second sleep.

Eddie flew the ship through the water, following the coordinates on his sensors. The facility wasn't far—only a few more minutes before he was close enough.

Less than a minute later the peak of the structure came into view. He could barely see it since the water was so thick and dark, and the base of the facility faded into the depths of the sea like nothing he'd ever seen before.

From what he *could* see this place was covered in some kind of reflective material, like that on the dome that covered the submarine. As the vessel sank lower, Eddie noticed that it was massive, probably as large as the *ArchAngel*.

Eddie located the tunnel for the second dry dock, which was a black opening in the side of the base. He propelled the submarine through it, hoping he didn't come across any other vehicles. Rex had said that the second dock was the least used, especially at this hour.

Eddie had no cloak, so if he was spotted it would mean a fight. Not much of a problem for him, but the easier this went off, the better.

After a moment, the light overhead indicated that he was in the base.

"What's your status, Blackbeard?" asked Julianna over the comm.

"I'm about to surface in Dry Dock Two," stated Eddie. The submarine rose, and to his relief the dock was deserted. There were a few submarines tied up along the dock, which relieved him since his submarine wouldn't stand out next to theirs. So far Rex's information had all been reliable.

Eddie turned off the engine and unlocked the hatch. "I'm about to enter the facility." He pulled the access badge that had been made by Chester from his pocket.

Julianna let out a sigh of relief. "Okay, but stay on the comm. Pip is already hooking into the network and trying to download files. There are a few more firewalls than we anticipated."

Eddie pulled out his gun before shoving the hatch open and climbing onto the dock. He headed to the exit and swung around the corner, and to his relief the long corridor, which featured stainless steel walls and blue-tiled floors, was empty. A blast of cold air made his teeth chatter —it was freezing on the other side of the door.

Soundlessly he made his way down the hallway, conscious that he would be trapped should anyone discover him here. He'd have preferred to have the personal cloaking technology on him, but Hatch had said he was running low on the crystals needed to power it. *Too bad,* thought Eddie. *Shit could've saved me some time.*

According to Rex the main lab was on the bottom level, which meant Eddie needed to take the stairs. He eyed the placard next to the first door he came to. The words were written in Trid, which was comprised of symbols Eddie didn't recognize. "Damn," he whispered, tapping his comm. "Marilla, what does the upside-down 'U' with a line through it mean?"

"Did you find something?" her voice chimed in. "That's storage, I believe."

"Right, okay," he said, walking steadily past it. "What about two 'Hs' on top of each other?"

"Bathroom," answered Marilla.

"Okay," he said, passing several doors and then taking a left. There was a single opening at the end of the short hallway. "Three 'Ls' in a diagonal?" he asked.

"Stairwell," said Marilla.

Eddie blew out a breath and pushed through the door. The stairwell was quiet and the air stagnant.

Pip's voice came over the comm. "I can't access the main network, which is where we suspect the information on the Brotherhood is being kept. Looks like you'll need to manually grant me access to the local network."

Eddie took the stairs two at a time. "Give me a minute."

"Beginning countdown," said Pip.

Eddie chuckled softly. "I didn't mean it literally."

The stairs ended abruptly at a single door. Bottom level.

"I'm here," said Eddie, trying to keep his breathing quiet.

"Perfect," said Pip. I have already scrambled the surveillance cameras." He paused. "And now I have access to the feed. You have three guards on that floor, patrolling."

"Sounds like I get to be the puppet on your strings, Pippy" said Eddie. "Tell me when to go. I'm ready."

"That's what I'm here for," said Pip. "The main server room is in the middle of that floor. All you have to do is run straight past a hallway on your left and then take the next door."

"Easy-peasy," said Eddie. He grabbed the door handle, but paused before opening it.

"On my signal, Blackbeard, begin sprinting at a moderate pace," said Pip. "Quietly enough to avoid detection, but faster than a jog. You'll have roughly ten seconds to make it to the door. Remember, that the area is locked, so have your access key ready."

Eddie turned the card around in his fingers. "Copy that."

A long moment of silence passed, during which Eddie thought his breath sounded too loud in the stairwell. Above him, a door opened and slammed shut. His best guess was three floors up, maybe four. "I've got company," he whispered.

"There's a guard in the main hallway right now," said Pip. "Please hold."

The thud of footsteps descending the stairs echoed downward. Eddie gripped his gun in one hand and stared up at the crack between the floors. He could make out a dark figure approaching, now two flights up. He pressed his lips together, keeping his breath steady.

"All clear. Go for it, Blackbeard," said Pip.

Eddie wheeled around and pulled the door back, then ran across the tile floor. In his peripheral vision he saw the back of a Trid guard, but Eddie quickly disappeared into another hall. He came to a halt in front of the server room door and waved the card across the reader, but a red light blinked back at him. *Damn it,* he thought, whipping his head toward the stairwell. Again he waved the card over the reader, with the same result.

"Two guards approaching from each side. They are about to flank you," said Pip.

He ran the key card again and it beeped too loudly—and then the green light flashed, a welcome sight to his eyes. Eddie yanked the door open and threw himself into the room as beads of sweat poured down his face.

"That was a close one," said Pip.

"You're telling me," whispered Eddie.

The main server room was dark and even colder than the rest of the frigid facility. Long rows of servers ran the length of the room, evenly dispersed. The only illumination was a line of blue lights above the servers.

"You're looking for a server marked with a backward 'K' next to a regular K," said Marilla, her voice surprising him. He'd almost forgotten she was there.

"Uhhh...any idea where to start?" asked Eddie, exchanging the access badge for a thumb-sized flashlight.

"Chester says that he suspects the Trid would put the one we want in the center of the room toward the back, but that's only a guess," said Marilla. "He admits he doesn't know."

"Got it. I'll start on this goose hunt," said Eddie as he strode down the center row, running his flashlight over the labels at the tops of the servers.

"I'm sorry to inform you," interjected Pip, "they've caught on to the scramble I placed on the surveillance. I believe they'll fully recover it soon."

"Which means I need to hurry my ass up. I get it." Spinning back and forth, Eddie checked the servers on either side of him as he progressed.

"More bad news," said Julianna.

"Do tell," said Eddie dryly.

"They found the submarine and are investigating it. Apparently it doesn't have Trid tags on it," said Julianna.

"Fuck, I'll get caught because I didn't register with the Trid government," said Eddie. "Bureaucracy *would* be the end of me. I should have fucking known."

"Right now they're just investigating it, but it might raise security alarms if we don't hurry. You'll have to get out of there another way," said Julianna.

"First I have to do what I came here to do." Eddie stopped in front of a server marked with the symbols Marilla had described. He pulled a drive from the pocket of his jacket and plugged it into the server. "Found the spot, and I'm using the manual override stick. Let's hope it works."

"Finally," breathed Julianna, relief in her voice.

The blue light on the server blinked several times as the drive initiated its override and Eddie tapped his foot, impatience almost overwhelming him.

"I'm in," Pip informed them. "I suggest escaping now."

"How exactly do you suggest I do that?" asked Eddie.

"Well, they are towing the unidentified submarine out of the base," said Julianna.

"They seem to fear it could have explosives on it," said Pip.

"That's a problem. How the fuck am I going to get out of here?" asked Eddie.

"I might have an idea," said Julianna, a cunning hint in her tone. "On my command, go back the way you came. Take the stairs up one floor, then use your access key to go straight through that door. That floor is empty."

Eddie grinned a bit. "You're being purposely mysterious."

"I might be. I've got a surprise for you," said Julianna, a smile in her voice.

Eddie paused at the door, waiting for Pip's signal.

"You ready?" said the AI. "You're only going to have a small window to make it through the hallway. Surveillance will come back on in thirty seconds."

"So no pressure, right?" asked Eddie.

"You love it and you know it," said Julianna.

"Okay, get ready to run," informed Pip. "Three, two..." There was a pause. "One. Go now."

Eddie whipped open the door and sprinted through the hall toward the stairwell. He was only a few meters away when Pip's voice burst into his ear. "Trid are descending the stairs, so turn and go the opposite direction. There's another stairwell on other side of hallway."

When Eddie skidded to a halt and twisted around his feet nearly slipped out from underneath him, but after recovering his balance he pushed harder. He realized he was going to run out of time to make it out of the hallway unspotted.

"Security camera feed reinstated in five, four, three, two, one," informed Pip.

Eddie didn't dare respond, opting to continue running, his feet pushing hard off the floor. He passed the hallway on the left and kept going, and spied a Trid guard down the hall, this time facing him.

"Hey, you! S-stop right there!" yelled the Trid.

Red lights flashed overhead and a siren blared.

"I've been spotted," said Eddie, yanking the door open.

"You think?" asked Julianna.

A cacophony of thundering footsteps echoed down the stairwell. The guards had been released to search for him, but thankfully most were on other decks. Eddie sprinted up the stairs, pulling the access badge from his pocket. He had it ready when he arrived.

The door he'd just come through opened, and he heard the stomping of bustling feet.

"Intruder! Stop!" yelled a Trid guard.

Eddie ran the access key over the badge reader, but it blinked red.

"They've locked down their security," informed Pip. "Looks like the access key won't work."

Eddie yanked his eyes up at the thundering of racing soldiers above him and edged over to the crack where he could see the stairs below. "I'm kind of a sitting duck here."

"One moment," said Pip. "Attempting lock override."

"Hurry!" ordered Eddie. He held up his pistol and aimed it downward, waiting for the guard to hit the landing to the next set of stairs. As soon as he did Eddie fired two shots, one of them knocking the guard to the floor.

Above him, the guards halted. Shots were fired toward Eddie through the opening.

He sank back flush to the wall. Below him the door to the first floor had opened again, and this time pounding footsteps followed. He couldn't get off a shot at the approaching guards like before, not without being spotted from above.

He raised his weapon, aiming it at the ascending stairs.

And the access scanner suddenly beeped behind him. "Override successful," said Pip.

"It's about time!" he barked, quickly pulling open the door.

When he entered, his eyes widened and his jaw dropped. It was the Trid's landing bay. Dozens of Stingrays sat in rows high above the water on multiple platforms, ready to be stolen.

13

Landing Bay, Pistris Base, Planet Kai, Tangki System

"Hot damn!" snapped Eddie, looking around the bay full of Stingrays.

"Surprise!" said Julianna over the comm.

"Badass!" he exclaimed, running over to the first of the many ships and climbing onto it. The door he'd just arrived through jerked as the guards tried to enter, and overhead the strobing red lights continued to swirl.

"They can't get through yet, but soon they'll have it open," said Pip, seemingly reading Eddie's mind.

"Hopefully I'll be out of here by then," he said pulling the door of the Stingray open. Compared to the submarine, this ship's cockpit was huge. He could thank the Trid for that, since they were slightly larger than humans and required the extra space.

"Think you can fly it?" asked Julianna.

"I think I can sure try," said Eddie, sliding into the seat and strapping himself in. The controls were similar to what he was used to, but he couldn't make heads or tails of the language. "Pip, buddy, I'm gonna need you to tell me which button makes this *go*."

"The green one, I believe," the AI informed him, "to the right of the control stick."

"The big one?" asked Eddie, spotting it immediately.

"Correct," said Pip.

Eddie pressed the button and the ship came alive, humming gently and vibrating his seat before settling into a smooth rhythm. "Yes!" he exclaimed. "Okay, now let's see about launching this thing."

"Getting out of here will be like entering the dry dock," explained Julianna over the comm.

"Which means I have to figure out how to make this baby swim," said Eddie, running his fingers over the dashboard. He hit a blue button, releasing a small missile which hit the row of Stingrays across the bay. The explosion sent a wave of water in his direction, and a burst of heat shot over him.

"Oops," he muttered.

"At least they can't follow you now," assured Julianna.

The door for the loading bay opened, and a horde of guards rushed through and took shelter behind a stack of crates on either side of the entrance. They were poised and ready to fire, probably trying to decide if they should launch an assault on their own ships.

Apparently the debate didn't last long, because a series of quick shots hit the side of the Stingray seconds later.

Eddie took the control stick in his hand and brought the Stingray forward, pulling it out of its position and wheeling it around to face the guards. He was in the open now, separated from the other ships. More shots were fired at him by the cluster of angry soldiers.

"Damn, boys," said Eddie. "I thought we could be friends." Eddie positioned the guns directly at one of the largest crates and tapped the blue button again, releasing another missile.

It hit the target, sending debris into the air. The guards leaped out of the way as fragments hit the platform.

"All right, enough fun for you," said Julianna. "Get the fuck out of there. You're going to have company soon, and not just a bunch of inexperienced guards with no combat experience."

"Copy that, Strong Arm." Eddie pivoted the Stingray, loving how it turned on a dime. He was slammed back into his seat as it sped forward and accelerated quickly. The spacecraft lifted off the runway, which narrowed ahead and took a sharp turn downwards into the water.

"You figure out how to make that craft swim yet?" asked Julianna.

Eddie's eyes scanned the controls. "No, someone told me to leave before I had a chance."

"Do you see a button with three 'Ts' in a row on it?" asked Marilla.

Eddie angled the craft and took the downward tunnel. Ahead, the surface of the blue water shimmered. As he expected, the landing bay was set up just like the dry dock.

He ran his eyes over the dashboard. "Yes, I have a button like that."

"Hit that. It means 'swim' in Trid," said Marilla.

Eddie was approaching the water quickly. "Here goes nothing." He pressed the button seconds before diving straight down. The ship didn't slow as he expected, but continued to race forward like a submarine with boosters. He took a turn and saw the expanse of the ocean ahead so he increased his acceleration again and burst out the tunnel, pulling the nose up to reach the surface. The Stingray was fast and bubbles raced over it as he flew up. He broke the surface seamlessly, switching to flying in the air as gracefully as he had in the water.

"Woohoo!" yelled Eddie. "Papa's got a new ride!"

"That's you?" asked Julianna.

"Yeah, I'm the hottie in the Stingray," said Eddie. Beside him the Q-Ship materialized, uncloaking.

"Welcome back, Blackbeard. Good work," said Julianna, pacing him.

"Good work, team. I couldn't have made it out of there without you all," said Eddie.

"Let's make for base. I have a feeling we're going to have some Trid on our ass otherwise," said Julianna.

"Copy that," said Eddie.

Loading Dock 01, QBS *ArchAngel*, Tangki System

Julianna strode over to the Stingray as it docked inside *ArchAngel* and waited for Eddie to pop out. As he opened the hatch he realized he was getting a fair amount of attention from the crew, who were rushing over to assist with the ship.

"You nearly got shot at, flying that thing in here," said Julianna, a mischievous smile on her face.

"Let me guess: you considered not informing Arch-

Angel it was me, didn't you?" asked Eddie, sliding down to the ground.

"I considered it," she teased.

"Well, thanks for letting her know I wasn't an enemy aircraft," said Eddie, admiring the ship.

"What in the *hell?*" a voice boomed from the other side of a row of cargo pods. They hadn't been there before.

Hatch wheeled around, his eyes wide as he took in the Stingray on the loading dock.

"Where the hell did you get that?" he asked, bustling over, his tentacles waggling in the air.

Eddie rubbed the wing with the side of his hand. "'I stole it, of course.'"

Julianna turned to Hatch with a proud look on her face. "You wanted blueprints for the Stingray to understand their construction, so we did you one better and brought you an actual ship."

Hatch, to their surprise, didn't look happy. "What were you thinking?! You idiots! You brought that thing into *ArchAngel?*"

"Well, yeah. It was kind of my getaway ride," admitted Eddie, confusion covering his face.

"We have trackers on our ships. Don't you think that the Trid will use the same technology?" asked Hatch.

Eddie's and Juliann's expressions went slack. "We didn't consider that, Hatch," said Julianna.

"I guessed as much." Hatch turned to the crew standing idly behind him. "Okay, children, listen up! We're looking for a tracker. I want you dimwits to sweep the entire ship for anything that might fit that description." Each crew member nodded and sprang forward to begin working on the ship.

"Sorry, Hatch," said Julianna. "We thought we were making your job easier by bringing back the ship."

Hatch's frown softened and he waved a tentacle at her. "It's fine. You did good, Julie. Once the chip is found and destroyed we'll be fine. *ArchAngel* will just have to take us through a gate to throw the Trid off, in case they *are* on our trail."

Eddie and Julianna waited for several minutes while the crew continued to examine the ship, carefully sweeping it and removing parts.

"Found it!" a crew member finally said from inside the cockpit. He raised a hand, showing a small chip with several wires sticking out of it.

"Keep searching, there might be more than one," commanded Hatch. He shook his head, obviously not impressed, then turned and pursed his mouth at Eddie. "Where's my submarine, Teach?"

Eddie threw out his arm at the Stingray. "Buddy ol' pal, I brought you a Stingray. Now you'll have the technology to make crafts that fly under water. Isn't that great?"

Hatch interwove two tentacles in front of his chest and stiffened. "Where. Is. My. Submarine?"

"About that... The thing is, that you forgot to put registration tags on it for the Trid government. Sooooo...." said Eddie, cringing a bit in anticipation of the explosion that was about to happen.

"Me? You're going to blame this on me? You lost my submarine, didn't you?" yelled Hatch.

"Let's say it was detained," said Eddie. "How about I buy

you a new submarine, or whatever it is that you want."

Hatch puffed up his cheeks, smoldering anger on his face.

"He *did* bring you the Stingray, and he couldn't have done that if he had returned in the submarine. So we had a loss and a major gain," said Julianna.

Hatch softened slightly. "I guess that's true," he muttered, pausing for a moment. "Fine, Julie, I'll let this one pass. But not again, Teach!"

One of the cargo pods, which had been resting on the other side of the bay, unloaded a small vehicle with wheels. It wasn't a ship, Eddie quickly realized, but some other kind of craft.

The car that backed out of the first cargo pod was a black convertible with orange flames around the headlights and body.

Eddie halted, and his mouth dropped open. "Is that… Oh, boy! That's…" His voice trailed away, stunned.

Hatch smiled, looking proud. "Look, Teach, but don't touch."

"You've got to be fucking kidding me, Doc. That's a custom-built 1949 Mercury Series 9CM like the one in the movie *Grease*, isn't it?" said Eddie.

Hatch shook his head. "Not 'like.'"

Eddie's mouth widened and he pointed, unable to say anything.

"Oh good, he's finally speechless," said Hatch as another custom car backed out of a second cargo pod. "Be careful. Reverse it out straight, not so close to the walls. You're going to scratch the paint."

"Is this your personal collection?" asked Julianna, hands

clasped behind her back.

"That it is. I thought I should have my cars with me, since I figure I'm going to be here for a while," said Hatch.

"What about your wives and kids?" asked Eddie.

"What about them?" asked Hatch.

Eddie shook his head. "Don't you miss them?"

"The kids are grown," said Hatch. "And the wives…" He waddled over to the nearest vehicle, gently touching its fine coat of red paint. "They just don't compare."

Before them now sat four antique hot rods, all in pristine condition. A fifth one backed out of the final cargo pod and smoothly pulled up next to the others.

"That's what I'm talking about," said Hatch loudly to the crew bustling around the cars, pointing a tentacle at the car. "That's how you pull a car out of a cargo pod. *Evenly*, so you don't risk nicking the paint."

The crew all kept their eyes down but nodded. Hatch was already mumbling under his breath about how they were all useless when the fifth car, a 1948 Ford De Luxe, drove up and the engine turned off. The driver's door opened, and to Eddie's surprise Knox stepped out.

"Hey, Gunner! What are you doing here?" asked Eddie.

He smiled widely, his eyes swiveling to the Stingray in the distance and then back to Eddie and Julianna. "You're back. Hey!"

"I asked Knox to help me unload the cars, since he showed interest in the inventory when I told him about it. Turns out the kid can actually drive, unlike these other numbskulls." Hatch had said the last part loudly to ensure the crew heard him.

"I'd love to take a look under hoods of these beauties,"

said Knox to Hatch.

A grin unlike anything Eddie had ever seen on Hatch's face spread on his mouth. "You ain't seen anything like these engines! Pristine. And the mechanicals are fascinating. They were done right, not cutting any corners." Knox and Hatch walked off, both gawking.

"Eddie?" called Julianna with a strange tension in her voice.

He turned to her. "What's up, Jules?"

"Pip has informed me that a ship has docked with Arch-Angel. He says there's a visitor aboard who is here to see me at your request. Do you know anything about that?"

Eddie dropped his gaze to the ground. "Oh, that. Right. Yes, I might have scheduled a meeting."

"A meeting with whom?" asked Julianna, instantly skeptical.

"It's more of a family reunion. I thought it was time we hashed out some issues," said Eddie, striding in the direction of the docking bay and pulling Julianna reluctantly with him.

"Issues? I don't know what you mean," she said, resisting but still coming along.

"I believe you when you say that, because you haven't been quite honest with yourself. That much I know," said Eddie, pressing the button to open the docking bay door. The connector between the dock and the visitor ship had already been secured.

"Are you intentionally trying to be vague?" asked Julianna, a line wrinkling the space between her eyes.

"Remember when you led me to the Trid loading dock, saying you had a surprise for me?" asked Eddie.

"That was less than an hour ago, so yes," said Julianna.

"Well, I have a surprise for *you*." Eddie turned and faced her directly, a serious look in his eyes. "I think Pip evolving to AI has brought up some things for you. Don't be mad—I'll deal with it—but I took it upon myself to call an old friend of yours. I think you two need to talk."

Julianna's eyes widened with surprise. "You didn't?"

Eddie nodded. "I did. He's waiting for you right through there." He indicated the connector opening, through which a research vessel's hatch could be seen in the distance.

"But..." said Julianna, voice trailing away. Her face slumped and her eyes drifted. Eddie had expected shock and rage, but instead there was...something else. Worry. Concern. Maybe even sorrow.

"It's fine, Strong Arm. You got this. Just go talk to him," said Eddie.

Julianna swallowed. Nodded. She tore her gaze in the direction of the ship, still hesitating.

"When you get back we'll have a drink to celebrate a successful mission," encouraged Eddie.

Julianna strode for the connector, but turned back before she entered it. "When I get back I'm going to break your nose."

Without another word, Julianna spun and went through the connecting airlock, undoubtedly aware of who she was going to meet.

Eddie watched with a swell of pity in his heart. Not for himself, of course, but for the friend he had just sent to meet her demons. For the ageless soldier who marched toward the truth.

14

Docking Bay, QBS *ArchAngel*, Tangki System

Do you know what this is about? Julianna asked Pip.

Silence.

Pip? What's going on?

Pip is not available right now. If you leave your name and message at the beep, he'll get back to you as soon as possible.

Oh, okay. Now I have two noses to break.

Julianna turned the lever on the front of the ship's hatch. She knew, absolutely *knew*, who she'd find inside this ship. Even so, she couldn't understand how she'd arrived at this point. When and why had Eddie set all this up? He had mentioned Pip's ascendance, so had that been it? Had she showed too much of her discomfort with that situation, however inadvertently?

Please try not to be angry at us.

This is about you becoming sentient. I get it.

Actually, you *don't* get it. This isn't about me at all, said Pip.

Fuck, you and Teach are talking in riddles. I'm in the freaking Twilight Zone, aren't I?

Julianna stepped over the ship's threshold and closed the door behind her. It was dark mostly, the gray light from overhead making everything appear to be black and white.

Oh, lookee there! Hatch needs my help with something incredibly important.

Pip... warned Julianna.

Monumental, actually. Super-important issue that only I can assist with. I think you'll be fine here without me.

Julianna gritted her teeth. She'd been set up. Why hadn't she gotten wind of this before now? She strode into the main area of the research vessel, which was empty— not a person in sight. However, she knew that wasn't really true.

"Hello, Ricky Bobby," said Julianna, her voice sounding strange in the empty ship.

The monitors around the ship flickered, flipping through different images and settling on a soft, calming blue. It was her favorite color, and he still remembered. Remembered that the hue relaxed her.

"Hello, Commander Julianna Fregin. It has been a long time," said the voice of the AI from overhead.

His voice was calming to her, and a touch of familiarity, of nostalgia, pulled her into a sea of memories. She pushed them aside—a practice she had become quite adept at—and focused on this moment and nothing else. "What brings you to the *ArchAngel*?" she asked, staring at the large display screen. Even as Julianna asked the question she regretted it, since she knew what this was about.

"I was asked here by Captain Teach," responded Ricky Bobby. "I believe he is a friend of yours."

Some friend, she thought, and was surprised at herself. She knew Eddie had done this with nothing but the best of intentions, yet she felt anger as she stood in this place listening to her old partner speak.

"How have you been?" she asked, not knowing what else to say. She swung her arms back and forth, nervously. This was dumb. Why should she be nervous around Ricky Bobby, her first EI? The two had been paired for a long time, until…

"I am well," said Ricky Bobby. "My research has led to many advancements for the Federation since last we saw each other. I've had many breakthroughs that I believe will assist future generations. In this I feel quite fulfilled, that my work shall go on to help others."

Julianna smiled as the rush of memories came back to her, sparked by the AI's philosophical nature. She enjoyed the notion that her old friend had made such an impact. Following that was disappointment, when she realized she hadn't been there to witness it.

"Is it true that you're commanding a squadron for the Federation?" asked Ricky Bobby.

"It's top secret, but yeah, it's true," said Julianna.

"Your secret is safe with me, as all your secrets always were," said Ricky Bobby.

Julianna's chest tightened. She didn't know how to respond to that. To any of this. There was something she was supposed to say here, but she didn't know how to begin.

"You sent me away," said Ricky Bobby.

There it was.

The words seemed to come from nowhere, like a blade to her chest spilling her soul. She wanted to scream. It hurt her badly, because it was the raw and ugly truth. Her greatest regret, and the worst mistake of her life.

This was why she was here. It was the reason Eddie had called Ricky Bobby and asked him to come. It was the secret she had kept from everyone she'd come into contact with ever since then.

And there would be no running away. Julianna would rather face a dozen armed Brotherhood soldiers than this conversation, but she had to.

"I know. And you went. We parted ways without any questions," said Julianna.

"You didn't want me to ask any questions," said Ricky Bobby matter-of-factly.

"You were better suited for research. Once you became sentient, you weren't going to be happy going on missions with me." She threw her arm in the direction of the *Arch-Angel*. "You wouldn't be happy being with me leading Ghost Squadron."

"You can't know what would make me happy. I think the real issue was that once I became sentient you didn't want me anymore," said Ricky Bobby.

He had always been that way—frustratingly blunt.

"That's not true, it's just that I thought we would be better off apart," said Julianna.

"You're paired with Pip now, correct?" asked Ricky Bobby.

"What about it?" she shot back, frustration in her voice. Her emotions were beginning to leak out despite herself.

"And he's become sentient, I've heard," said Ricky Bobby.

"Yeah, apparently I develop AIs. You're welcome." She faked a laugh, but it sounded all wrong.

"How do you feel about him now?" asked Ricky Bobby.

"I don't feel anything about it or him. Why should I care?" Julianna was close to screaming, which meant that she was close to telling the truth, and it scared her.

"Jules, talk to me," said Ricky Bobby, and then added, "Please?"

Julianna threw herself into a chair and let out an exasperated breath. She studied the space, which was filled with files and artifacts—all things Ricky Bobby had created or found during his research.

"It was easier when you were an EI," she said after a long moment.

"Because?"

"Because I've been here for a long time and lost a lot. As soon as you evolved, became sentient, it worried me. You were real all of a sudden. You were someone I could care about. Someone I could lose," said Julianna, the words rushing out of her unrehearsed.

"So you sent me away," said Ricky Bobby.

She slowly nodded. "When you evolved it worried me. You were all of a sudden real. It meant you had a soul. It meant you could die."

"So," said Ricky Bobby, "the truth comes out at last."

She dropped her head. "I did what I thought was best for both of us. I was a combat pilot, and I could have died at any time. Hell, I still can. That's the nature of the job. I couldn't let you see that, experience it. You were like a newborn, just coming into your new life. If you'd watched me die... I just... I couldn't let it happen."

"And now that you have another AI, what do you want to do?" asked Ricky Bobby.

Julianna stared around, not really seeing. "I'm not sure. I can't keep pushing everyone away, I guess. It's ridiculous."

"I understand your position, Jules," said Ricky Bobby, his voice sensitive.

"I figured you would. You were always good like that."

"You did send me away because you thought it was best for me, but you also thought it was best for you," said Ricky Bobby.

Julianna pressed her lips together, unsure what to say.

"I don't blame you. You were protecting yourself, but you should have known that no one can protect you better than your AI. Most don't know the honor of having one AI, and you've now had two. You, Jules, are a truly remarkable individual," said Ricky Bobby. He was so wise. Not just intelligent, like most AIs, but wise in his own way, with an intuitive spirit.

"Ricky..." she began, then let his name hang in the air.

"Yes, Jules?"

"I'm sorry," said Julianna simply.

"Don't be. You did what you thought was right. When we know better, we do better," said Ricky Bobby.

"Yeah," she said, mostly to herself. And accepting Pip had been the right thing to do. He was her friend now, not just an EI. She worried how that would change things. She worried about losing him, but what was the point if there was nothing at stake? She was fighting for the Federation for that exact reason. The best things in life were worth fighting for.

"My research has taken me all over, Jules," Ricky Bobby started. "I love my work, as you well know, but it is very lonely. And it has helped me to understand what's important, more important than scientific breakthroughs."

"What's that?" asked Julianna.

"Friendship. That's more important than anything else," said Ricky Bobby.

Julianna leaned back in the seat, experiencing a new pressure in her chest. She nodded, then felt the weight whisk away with each new breath. "Yes, I think you're right."

She couldn't help but lament how she had treated Pip. He was her friend, not just as an AI but as someone more. Part of her worried how that new perception would change things. She didn't want to lose him like she had Ricky Bobby or her long-deceased friends, but what was the point in living so long if you didn't have connections with other people? She was fighting for the Federation to preserve its people, their bonds, their families. If she couldn't let herself be a part of that experience, how could she claim to defend it?

The truth of the matter was that she had chosen this life, chosen to be alone. No matter what Ricky Bobby told her she knew that their separation had been her doing, but after all this time she could rectify that mistake.

"You *are* right. Maybe you can check in with us from time to time, help us with some projects," said Julianna.

"I'd like that very much, Jules. I like to help my friends."

Julianna didn't want to punch Eddie so much anymore, or Pip for that matter. She wasn't going to tell them they were right, but she was glad that they'd cared enough to intervene. For too long she'd carried this baggage, but now she could let it go.

"Ricky Bobby?" said Julianna, waiting for his reply.

"Yes, Jules?"

"I've missed you," she said plainly.

"And I you."

15

Intelligence Center, QBS *ArchAngel*, Tangki System

Chester wadded up a sticky note and tossed it through the air, and it lodged in Marilla's long brown hair. She didn't bother looking at him, just blew out an annoyed sigh and kept her eyes pinned on her computer screen. This girl could focus harder than anyone, which was probably why she had a slew of degrees and more knowledge of alien species than anyone Chester had ever met. He'd never been one for formal education, which had been fine back when he lived alone and spent his evenings behind his bedroom computer, but now, sitting here beside her, it made him feel inferior. Not in any major way, of course. He was still the supreme hacker, according to the Dark Web. No one could match him, not even the Federation boys with their fancy diplomas from look-at-me institutes.

He swallowed, his throat somewhat dry, and asked, "Did you miss me while you were gone?"

Marilla lifted her gaze and regarded him thoughtfully

for a moment before untangling the wadded paper from her hair. "If I say 'yes,' will you stop throwing things at me?"

He pulled another sticky note from the surface of his desk and crumpled it. They pretty much lined the entire surface, not to mention the many computer screens in front of him. "That's not how this works," he teased. "We're honest with each other. You're not supposed to tell me something because it's what you think I want to hear, and I don't stop bugging you just because you give me lip service. We're legitimate with one another." He threw the paper ball, but missed her this time.

Marilla lifted an eyebrow, looking curious. "Do you write out these little speeches beforehand?"

"Yes, and I practice them in the mirror after I shower and before I shave," said Chester, then added, "while all I'm wearing is a towel."

She dropped her gaze to her computer screen as if suddenly engrossed in her work again.

"Are you picturing me wearing nothing but a towel wrapped tightly around my waist?" asked Chester.

Her cheeks reddened, but only briefly. "I'm confused," she said. "I didn't think you needed to shave."

Chester turned around and stared at the screen. It was true that he had a baby face, with his fair skin and lightly-colored spiky hair. He couldn't help it, and he wouldn't apologize for being so devilishly handsome.

He rubbed his smooth chin. "You can lie to yourself, Mar, but you can't lie to *me*. You'll never erase the visual of me standing half-naked in front of the mirror rehearsing the things I'm going to say to you later. It's all you'll think about. You'll be obsessed with me."

"Boy, *I* already am," said the Captain's voice from the door.

Chester spun to find Eddie standing squarely in the doorway with a smile on his face. The guy was always smiling. *He probably grinned while beating up bad guys and sported a toothy smile as he delivered one-two punches*, Chester thought, amusing himself with the idea.

"I was able to crack the data Pip sent over to me. Most of it was encoded, but the Trid aren't as clever as they think they are—or maybe it's just that I know all their tricks now," said Chester.

"Which is exactly why I'm obsessed with you," said Eddie, striding into the room. He pulled out a chair and sat down in it backward, leaning toward Chester over the back support.

Harley peeked his head out from beside Marilla's desk, yawning, then stretched and made his way over to Eddie. The Captain bent down and scratched the dog behind the ears.

"As you should be. You know a good thing when you see it," said Chester. His gaze drifted to Marilla, who was pretending not to pay attention.

"You've had the data for a whole hour and you've already cracked it," said Eddie, then looked at Marilla and pointed in Chester's direction. "That's definitely why I love this guy."

Chester turned back to his computer and pulled up the data from Pistris Station. "I was able to track down the scientists who designed the Stingrays."

Eddie shook his head. "We don't need that information anymore. I stole one of the bad boys, so no need for the plans."

A Cheshire-cat grin spread on Chester's mouth. "I heard a rumor about this Stingray trying to enter the loading bay. You nearly got shot down."

"Nearly." Eddie laughed.

"Regardless, hearing about it got me thinking," Chester continued. "Sometimes I get obsessed with information, you know? I just start looking into things one bit of data at a time. It's obsessive, I get that, but every once in a while it leads to something interesting. In this case I decided to research the origin of Stingray ships, so I looked into the scientist who designed them, the one who originally built that model. Turns out he's also the same person who built another ship not too long ago, the *Unsurpassed*."

"*Unsurpassed*," mused Eddie, stroking his jaw.

"Yeah. I dug a bit deeper when I found the name, because it seemed interesting and something about it caught my eye. I found that it was commissioned by an anonymous client awhile back," explained Chester. "But that's not even the weirdest part. Something about it felt off, and you know—after I found that out I couldn't stop digging. I had to know the whole story."

Eddie nodded. "And?"

Chester smirked. "I followed the money trail through several fake accounts until it brought me to the end. You wouldn't believe the amount of work it took, but I was in deep already so I couldn't stop—not when I'd come this far."

"So who was it?" asked Eddie, his curiosity totally piqued.

"Mr. Felix Castile," Chester said, cocking his head, not afraid to show his pride. "You can imagine my surprise."

Eddie leaned forward, his eyes widening as he rocked the chair up on two legs. "No way!"

Chester pulled up an image of the massive ship on the main screen. "It appears to be Felix's personal carrier."

"Whoa, that baby is sweet," said Eddie, gawking at the image. The ship was smaller than the *ArchAngel*, but still had launch tunnels and a large landing bay. Federation ships were generally considered the greatest in the galaxy, but this *Unsurpassed* ship certainly gave some a run for their money.

Chester swiped his finger on the screen in front of him and brought up the blueprints. "It's not Federation technology, but from what I can deduce it's pretty impressive. The ship you encountered before seems to have been a prototype for this. It was similar in many respects, but this one is bigger and tougher and has plenty more cannons to kill you with."

"Then I can only imagine what kind of technology *Unsurpassed* uses. Please send this over to Hatch. I want to get his take on this," said Eddie.

"Already done." Chester pushed his glasses up on his nose, suppressing a proud smile.

"Of course it is," said Eddie, turning to Marilla. "This guy always exceeds expectations. Don't you just love him?"

Marilla's cheeks blushed pink and she nodded, then squinted at her computer screen like something had just grabbed her attention.

"Yeah, Mar, don't you just love me? Maybe that's too strong of a word. Can't get enough of me, perhaps? Completely smitten with me, possibly?" teased Chester.

She looked up, her mouth popping open. "What? Are you talking to me? Sorry, I was distracted."

"*Sure* you were." Chester nodded, eyes laughing. "Anyway, Captain, I was able to track down the location for this scientist who designed Felix's ship. I figured that if we could talk to him we might be able to learn what other technology Felix has commissioned. Technology developments always lead to motives and plans."

"Good thinking. That's exactly right," agreed Eddie. "Who is this guy, and *where* is he?"

"Deacon Flick—that's the guy's name. And you're not going to believe this, but he's hiding right under the Federation's nose." Chester pulled up a document, and enlarged the text of a location.

"Onyx Station? You've got to be kidding me," said Eddie, reading the information.

"Yep. The scientist responsible for designing ships for the enemy is hanging out on our home turf." Chester clicked his tongue three times and shook his head.

"Mr. Flick is about to get a surprise visit," said Eddie. He stood and patted the dog, who was dutifully lying next to him.

When he strode for the exit, Harley followed.

16

Loading Bay, QBS _ArchAngel_, Onyx Station, Paladin System

The scraggly mutt bounded at Julianna when she entered the loading bay early. She figured that Teach would be prepping before they set out. She'd noticed that he was always early, using the time to mentally prepare before each mission. They hadn't spoken since he'd dropped the Ricky-Bobby bomb on her. Actually she was pretty certain he was avoiding her, since he'd relayed the information on Deacon Flick and the trip to Onyx via ArchAngel.

Harley had a disgusting saliva-covered bone-thing in his mouth. She peered down at him and shook her head.

"He wants you to throw it," said Eddie. He knelt, knees splayed wide.

"I know what he wants, but I don't want to touch that slobber-soaked bone," said Julianna.

Eddie whistled and the dog trotted over to him, for

which Harley received a pat on his head. He dropped the bone in front of Eddie, and the pilot picked it up and threw it down the empty expanse of the loading bay. "I think you *do* want to play with Harley, but it's kind of like the Ricky Bobby situation."

"I had no idea that you didn't value your life and wanted me to end it," said Julianna coolly.

"When someone ends me, it's probably going to be you. You're unmatched, and could have me at your mercy without breaking a sweat." Eddie looked after the dog with a satisfied smile on his face, as if he'd just thought of something pleasing. "What a way to go—at the hands of the great Commander Fregin!"

Julianna rolled her eyes. "Since when have you thought that intervening in my affairs was a good idea? Was this a plan you hatched while you were drunk?"

Harley had returned with the bone and stubbornly dropped it in front of Julianna again, but she simply shook her head at him.

"I just spotted an opportunity for closure and yes, I meddled a bit in your affairs. I'm not sorry about it, so if you want to kick my ass I'll take it like a man." Eddie pushed to his feet, knee popping as he did. He shook out his leg as if it had cramped from his kneeling position.

"I'm not mad at you, Teach. I have every right to be, but I get that you were trying to help," said Julianna. Harley picked up the bone again and brought it to Eddie, from whom he immediately got what he wanted.

"I knew you were a reasonable and tolerant person, but now I realize you're understanding as well," said Eddie as Harley bounded after the soggy missile.

"You could have told me that you were trying to set up a meeting with Ricky Bobby," said Julianna.

You would have threatened to kill him, said Pip in her head.

"You would have put me in a headlock so fast," said Eddie, "or worse."

Julianna smiled. "That's what Pip says too."

"Ha! And he knows you better than anyone else."

"It's true, but you knew me well enough to know that Pip's evolution had brought up old concerns of mine. You might pretend to be a good ol' boy, but I think you hide intuition," said Julianna.

Eddie shrugged, his eyes on Harley, who had dropped the bone once more at Julianna's feet. "I just wanted to help my *friend*. You had the opportunity to easily resolve things with Ricky Bobby, which is not an option for some people. Sometimes we can't go back and say we're sorry for walking away. We can't always say goodbye to the people we love."

Julianna could hear...something...in the way he spoke. His tone had shifted and became almost distant. He seemed to retreat inside himself a bit—a reaction she knew quite well herself—and she saw a shadow in his eyes, possibly a memory of sorts. "You're talking like you know this from experience," she finally said.

Eddie snapped his fingers to get Harley's attention, but this time the dog stayed in front of Julianna, his tongue hanging out of his mouth and eyes looking expectantly up at her.

"Maybe I do and didn't get a chance to say goodbye, or maybe I'm okay, or I messed up," said Eddie, walking over.

He paused when he was right in front of Julianna, a strange seriousness on his usually-smiling face.

She twitched from the emotion in his eyes and how it plainly spoke of something more. Something deeper than anything she'd ever seen from him. She knew it was pain, the sort that lingers for a lifetime and doesn't let you go.

Slowly he leaned down and grabbed the bone. Then he straightened and threw it, but Harley didn't go after it. Instead he stayed there and stared up at Julianna the same way Eddie was staring.

"Are you referring to a girl? One who you let walk away?" asked Julianna.

Eddie shook his head with a tragic look in his eyes. "No, nothing like that. I'm referring to my parents."

Julianna swallowed, her throat tight. "And now you regret not dealing with things before it was too late, is that right?"

"I regret thinking there would always be time to go back and fix everything," said Eddie, his eyes skipping to the poor dog still sitting at their feet.

Eddie smiled abruptly and was suddenly his former self again, a joyful expression filling his bright face. He bent down over Harley, patting the dog's head. "One of these days she'll give you what you want," he said, looking up at Julianna. "Don't give up on her just yet."

The door to the hangar opened, and both Lars and Knox entered.

Julianna turned around to face them. A bandage was

wrapped around Knox's arm where he'd been shot. That kid hadn't complained about it at all, which made Julianna like him even more.

I believe you and the Captain just had a moment, said Pip.

I don't know what you mean.

I have a transcript of the conversation. Would you like me to run back through it for you?

I don't think that's necessary.

You should ask him more about his parents, Pip encouraged her.

If he wants to talk about them, he will.

Oh, right, wait for other people to open up first. No outward attempts on your part at deepening relationships.

Pip, are you trying *to get under my skin?*

The AI laughed in her head. **Under your skin! Good one, and no, I'm simply trying to point out that relationships are a two-way street.**

I can't believe you're lecturing me on relationships. I'll be perfectly fine without your input on the subject.

That's too bad then. I found a quiz from Cosmopolitan, a magazine from Earth. It's old, but I think the results would hold up. The quiz is entitled, "What's Your Relationship Style?"

This conversation is not *happening.*

I assure you that it is. I took the quiz and got "Clingy Codependent." I think my results are a bit flawed, based on my situation with you.

Julianna burst out laughing, which gained the attention

of the three men who were busy discussing the logistics of the mission.

The quiz classified you as a "Distant Heartbreaker." I took the quiz for you, based on how I suspected you'd answer. I calculated an eighty-five percent probability that I was correct. Would you like to take the quiz yourself to verify?

Hell no, I do not, and neither should you, Pip. Those quizzes are terrible.

Let me know if you change your mind. I also found many other useful quizzes like, "Does Your Hookup Want to be Your Boyfriend?" and "What's Your Ideal Sex Position?" For obvious reasons I couldn't complete the quizzes myself.

Oh, gross. You have way too much free time on your hands if you're taking quizzes from women's magazines, Pip. We really ought to find you something more productive to do.

Pip laughed again. **"Time on my hands."** *Hands...that's funny, Julianna.*

Eddie cleared his throat to get Julianna's attention. "Based on the distant look on your face, I'm guessing you're having a conversation with your favorite AI."

"I can hear you," said ArchAngel from overhead, butting into the conversation. "Honestly, there are too many AIs coming and going in my ship."

Eddie frowned. "Aw, Archie... You know you're my main squeeze, babe!"

"Apology accepted, Captain Teach," said ArchAngel, "but please, no nicknames for me."

Julianna couldn't help but laugh. "Yes, we're done. He's

apparently lost his damn mind and needs to be completely rebooted."

"**Lost my mind.**" **Another good one**, said Pip.

"Are you up to speed?" Julianna asked Knox and Lars.

They both agreed with a nod.

"Based on what happened last time in Gun Barrel, we think having you and Lars, join us will be smart. We don't want to get cornered again and be outnumbered," said Juilianna.

"I'm up for a mission," said Lars.

"All right, then let's suit up and get going," commanded Julianna.

Deck Twelve, Onyx Station, Paladin System

Eddie grinned when he saw his team.

Knox and Lars were already dressed, wearing the uniforms of Onyx Station's utility personnel crew. Thanks to the Federation's control of this station, acquiring them had been a simple task.

Julianna pulled the blazer on over her crisp white shirt. She looked different in slacks and a button-up blouse. Different in a good way, Eddie observed. She fastened a badge to the lapel of her jacket, straightening it.

"Stop staring," Julianna threatened when she caught him watching her.

He jerked his head down and bent over, pretending his shoe was untied. "I wasn't staring."

"If you think *I* look different dressed in civilian clothes, you need to look in the mirror," said Julianna.

"I can only imagine that I look a little stiff in this suit." Eddie straightened and smoothed his slacks.

"You definitely don't look like yourself, which is the point. If *I* can hardly recognize you, then the Brotherhood who might be hiding and waiting for us, won't notice you," said Julianna.

"You really think that the Brotherhood would be so brave as to come onto Onyx Station?" asked Knox.

Lars nodded, leaning on a mop he'd snagged. "The Brotherhood shouldn't be underestimated. I have no difficulty believing they could sneak onto this station if ordered to."

"There's so much going on here that it's not hard to get away with stuff," said Eddie. "Look at this Deacon Flick guy. This scoundrel is hiding right under our noses here."

Julianna picked up a clipboard that carried a stack of papers pinned together at the top. "All right, you guys, get into position. Teach and I will be right behind you. Comms on, everyone."

Knox and Lars saluted the Commander before leaving the room they'd secured for prep, which was a back room in the maintenance sector.

When the two had been gone for a minute Eddie said, "Gunner? Carnivore? Do you copy?"

"Affirmative," they said in unison over the comm.

"Keep your eyes open for suspicious people. Don't draw attention to yourself, and abandon position if you're identified. The last thing we need is any of this reflecting back on the Federation," said Julianna.

"Copy," said Lars.

Eddie buttoned his suit jacket, trying to look important.

He read Julianna's badge. "Ms. Donaldson, are you ready to embark on our census work for the station?"

Julianna smiled slightly. "Yes, Mr. Petersen. Let's go count heads."

The two strolled through the corridor of Deck Twelve with their chins held high. Beings of many races brushed by, most taking no notice of them in their official navy-blue suits. Both scanned the crowd as they passed for anyone who might be a Brotherhood soldier or Trid accomplice.

At a second-hand appliance store Eddie paused and put his back to the shop. On the other side was a laundromat. The lower deck was full of these rundown enterprises, and riff-raff to match.

Eddie pointed to the laundromat. "Sally, you want to take the laundromat? I'm overdue for a break."

Julianna pursed her lips, obviously not approving of how Eddie slacked off even when undercover. "Sure, Billy."

She entered the laundromat and started talking to the clerk at once, and Eddie surveyed the area around the second-hand appliance shop. Working around the passersby in front of it was Lars, pushing a mop. He kept his eyes down and was doing a great job of looking like a dejected custodian trying to work as people dirtied the floors behind him.

Knox had set up a ladder just in front of the next shop, and he opened a tool box to remove a bulb. People gave him space, not wanting to bump into the tall ladder.

Julianna returned with her clipboard clutched to her chest. "All done, Billy." She pointed at the second-hand retail shop. "Why don't we take this next one together?"

"Sounds good, Sal," said Eddie, sweeping his arm out to present the way to Julianna.

Unimpressed, she trotted off. Knox started climbing the ladder when they entered the store. A bell hummed marking their arrival, and an old woman with curly gray hair looked up from a tablet. Her eyes roamed over their suits and she pursed her lips.

"What do you want?" she asked impatiently. The shop was lined with shelves that held dusty old appliances, things Eddie hadn't seen in years and some he'd never run into before. The counter in front of her was glass, and was filled with odds and ends like toasters and old phones.

"Just a moment of your time, Ma'am. We're with the census department," said Eddie.

"I know who you're with. You say 'census,' but you mean 'taxes.' You just want to count us so we have to pay you," said the woman sternly.

Julianna raised her brow. "I didn't realize you had stopped using Onyx Station's infrastructure and were existing without any of its conveniences," said Julianna, a sharp tone in her voice.

Eddie gave her a warning look. "What I think my partner here was trying to say is, taxes ensure that you have the things you need."

The old woman narrowed her gray eyes at Julianna, wrinkles splaying around her tight mouth. "I don't think that was what she was trying to say."

Julianna cleared her throat and lifted her clipboard. "Can you confirm how many people work in this establishment?"

"Two," the woman said, sounding impatient.

"Names of Onyx residents, please?" Julianna pretended to be reading off the paper.

"Betsy McGuire and Deacon Flick. I work for him," said the woman.

"Yes, that confirms what we have here. I just need to have you, Betsy, sign here." Julianna handed the woman the clipboard and pointed to a line, handing her a pen.

With the same sour attitude as before, the woman took the pen and scratched her signature.

"And now we just need Mr. Flick's signature as well," said Julianna.

"Deacon is in the back working with some new customers," said the old woman. "I'll take the form back there."

Julianna shook her head. "We have to witness the signing."

"Can we go back there and get Mr. Flick's signature?" asked Eddie, trying to see what was in the rooms behind the counter. The place was so cluttered it was hard to see much of anything.

"I'm afraid you can't. It's a new client, and they've asked for privacy. Whatever they want repaired, they didn't even want me seeing it," said the woman, still sounding annoyed.

"I can't imagine that," muttered Julianna.

"Did you say there was a client?" asked Eddie. He glanced at Julianna, motioning with his eyes at the back room and hoping she took the hint.

Julianna turned her head to the side. Her eyes widened after a quick second of listening. "There's a struggle happening. We're going in." She shot around the old woman and sprinted for the back, with Eddie right behind her.

"Copy that," said Lars over the comm.

"You can't go back there," the woman yelled after them.

"Stay on alert," said Eddie to the two in position.

The back was dark and lined tightly with shelving. A single light shined over a main workstation, which was near the farthest wall. Slumped over one of the desks was a gray-haired man wearing a thick sweater, blood puddling under his mouth.

Julianna pulled her gun from her waistband, eyes alert, and Eddie did the same.

She backed up, scanning the darkened space, and with one hand she felt for Deacon Flick's pulse. After a moment, her gaze connected with Eddie and she shook her head. He was dead.

Felix had beaten them to it again.

Eddie began to open his mouth to speak, when suddenly something rustled behind the farthest shelf. Whoever had killed Deacon Flick was still there.

17

Deck Twelve, Onyx Station, Paladin System

Lars tightened his fingers around the mop in his hands as he stared around the busy lane. There were many races filing by. He felt awful that he was profiling, looking for Trid and Kezzin, but the fact remained that those were the races who would be working for the Brotherhood.

Knox shot him a tentative look from his position at the top of the ladder, from which he could see farther and spot any oncoming attacks. He pressed his chin into his chest and over the comm he said, "Carnivore, I've identified three Brotherhood soldiers at your three o'clock, approaching fast."

Lars pressed his boot down on the mop head and yanked the handle off as a loud commotion broke out down the lane. The crowd parted as the three Brotherhood soldiers pushed through, their gazes focused on the appliance store. They had to have been alerted to Julianna and Eddie's presence, so their people were in there.

Knox started down the ladder, still holding the bulb he'd changed out—or pretended to.

The Brotherhood soldiers charged, taking no notice of either Knox or Lars, and when they were next to the ladder Knox dropped the bulb. It shattered on the ground, and they jumped backward. They looked up, disgust written on their faces.

"Hey there!" yelled one of the soldiers.

"Oops," said Knox, holding up his hands.

The soldiers started forward again, and Knox picked up the toolbox balanced on the top of the ladder and turned it upside down. Tools rained from above, knocking two of the soldiers on the head, and they stumbled away.

"You!" yelled the one who was still standing.

"Oops," said Knox again, a coy look on his face.

Lars almost laughed. He liked this Knox character.

The soldier charged for the ladder, but Lars raised the handle that had been connected to the mop and slammed it across the male's chest, knocking him back.

The other soldiers had recovered and scrambled to their feet so Lars tried his best to intimidate them, brandishing the handle and spinning it through his hands like a baton. This gave the soldiers pause, but only for a moment. They whipped out guns, which made everyone nearby panic and retreat immediately. The authorities would be called now. They needed to get out of there before this caused too much attention.

Lar swung the staff at the soldiers again, and when they jumped backward he brought the handle down hard to knock the gun out of one of the males' hands.

Knox clambered to the ground to go after the gun, but the Brotherhood soldier dove for the ladder and knocked it over. Knox fell straight to the ground, a *crack* punctuating his landing.

Lars dropped the handle and pulled his own gun from where it was strapped to his ankle, aiming it at the solider with the gun, who by this time had swung around and aimed at him. The other solider was trapped under the ladder, and was scrambling to get out. Knox lay on the ground, grimacing as he reached for the gun only inches away. He got to it just in time, aiming it in turn at each of his opponents.

"Put it down," Lars ordered the Brotherhood soldier in front of him. There was a real fear in the male's eyes as he looked at his pinned buddy and then back at Lars. Then he sprinted straight down the lane, quickly getting lost in the crowd of onlookers, and Lars lowered his weapon, cursing beneath his breath.

Julianna wordlessly motioned to the right side of the shelves.

Eddie nodded, going to the left. They were almost to the shelf when it rocked forward an inch and then back, then crashed to the floor in front of them. Eddie shot backward out of the trajectory of the objects flying from the shelf as dust exploded and covered the room in a cloud. He lifted his gun, but couldn't see much through the haze.

"What's going on?" yelled the old woman.

Someone grabbed Eddie around his neck from behind and he grasped the arms, falling to his knees and flipping the large Brotherhood soldier over his back and straight to the ground. From the sound of it, Julianna was battling someone too.

The guy pushed to his feet and ran for the exit.

"We've got a runner," said Eddie over the comm.

"Two down out here," returned Lars.

Julianna fired and something fell to the ground.

Eddie sprinted after the fleeing soldier and when he was almost to the door at the front of the shop he dove and caught the Kezzin around the waist. The soldier fell hard, Eddie on his back.

The old woman screamed somewhere behind them, then picked up an appliance and threw it at them. The Kezzin rolled over, kicking at Eddie as he tried to get to his feet.

"Bad people! No!" yelled the woman from the side of the shop. When she picked up a toaster and launched it at them Eddie ducked, shielding his face with his arm.

She picked up a small TV and threw that too. It exploded, sending parts in all directions.

The Kezzin dashed for the door and Eddie took off after him, but a radio crashed into his back and knocked him to the side. The Kezzin flew through the door and slammed it behind him as Eddie went after him, but a hair dryer smashed into the closed door.

"I caught the one who just ran out!" barked Lars over the comm.

Eddie halted, bending over and taking a breath. He held

up his hand to the woman who had a breadmaker over her head in both hands, about to throw it too.

"Don't. I'm not the bad man," said Eddie.

Julianna ran to the front of the shop and looked around at the destruction. There was a question in her eyes as she eyed Eddie.

"I'm fine," he said in answer. "You?"

"I had to take that Kezzin out. No choice," said Julianna.

"OK," he said to Julianna. "We'll have someone come in and clean up this mess," said Eddie to the old woman. She still had the breadmaker in her hands, but didn't look as bent on throwing it.

The woman nodded, uncertainty and confusion in her eyes as she slowly lowered her arms.

Julianna steered the woman to the very front of the shop. "Stay up here. Someone will come to take away these males."

"Deacon... Is he?" The woman's question hung in the air.

"Yes, I'm afraid so. I'm sorry," said Julianna with rare sensitivity in her voice.

The woman nodded, her eyes on the floor, which was now littered with broken appliances. "I didn't think those Kezzin were customers, actually."

"Can you tell us anything about the work Deacon did away from this shop?" asked Julianna.

The woman brought her startled eyes up to Julianna's face. "Deacon didn't do any work away from the shop."

Julianna nodded. The woman didn't know anything. Deacon had kept this employee in the dark.

"Got the Brotherhood soldiers secured out here, but we need to get Knox to the infirmary," said Lars over the comm.

Eddie's eyes shot to the door, but he couldn't really make out much through the murky glass. "What's wrong with Knox?"

"He's fine, but it appears he's broken his foot," said Lars.

"First you were shot, and now you've broken your foot," said Eddie over the commotion in the bar. "Sure you want to stay on our team?"

Lars and Eddie had carried Knox to the infirmary while Julianna supervised the cleanup of the shop. They couldn't let anyone realize that the Federation—and Ghost Squadron specifically—had had anything to do with this, which meant there could be no evidence of their involvement.

An hour later Eddie had contacted her and said that Knox was all set, with orders from the doctor to stay off the foot and rest up. Then he'd told her to meet them at the Honky Tonk Bar on Deck Thirty. When Julianna had questioned the decision, Teach had stated that it would cheer Knox up. The guy indeed had a wide grin on his face as he polished off his second beer.

"You're not getting rid of me that easily. I don't care if I break every bone in my body. I wanna be a part of this team. I wanna do what you all do," said Knox.

Eddie, smiling, brought his mug of beer to his mouth. "Well, good. You did a damn good job today. You both did."

"Felix was one step ahead of us again," said Julianna, taking a sip. It burned her throat, but went down easy enough. They had the good stuff on Onyx.

"That fucker took out his own scientist!" said Eddie.

"What kind of person does that?" asked Lars.

"I have a feeling we're going to find out many despicable things about Felix Castile," said Eddie.

The commotion in the center of the bar, which resembled the inside of a barn, got louder. A ring had been framed in the main area and a mechanical bull stood in the center of its padded floor.

A man pushed up from the ground, having just been bucked off.

"Jules, you want to ride the bull first or shall I?" asked Eddie.

"I'm not riding it at all," said Julianna.

"But it will cheer Knox up! He broke his foot. Don't you want to make him feel better?" asked Eddie.

Julianna looked at Knox.

"It's true, Commander," he said. "I can't think of anything that would make me happier than watching you two tackle the bull. We never got a chance to do any real cowboy stuff in Gun Barrel."

"I ate a bunch of sand. Does that count?" asked Eddie.

"It doesn't," said Julianna. "How about whoever loses a bet on the Captain rides?"

Eddie pushed to his feet and puffed his chest out. "Fine with me, as long as there's a double show."

Julianna looked at Lars, who was grinning. "Lars, what do you think?"

"I'm game for that. I think he'll make it eight seconds on the first round," said Lars.

Julianna set her glass down. "I bet on six seconds."

"You both disappoint me greatly, but the loser is up next," said Eddie, grabbing the beer and chugging the rest. He wiped his mouth with his sleeve, then smacked his chest. "Get ready to be impressed! And remember, loser goes next." Eddie smirked as he walked toward the bull.

They watched Eddie as he headed off to sign up for the event, then Knox turned to Lars with a smirk on his face. "You and the Commander bet on the Captain often?"

Lars shifted his gaze to Julianna, who was watching Eddie throw his leg over the bull's side. Lars nodded. "So far I've won all the rounds."

Julianna tilted her head in Eddie's direction. "Yeah, but this time the win is mine. Be prepared to ride that bull."

"You seem confident, Commander," said Lars, curious.

Her drink in her hand, Julianna pointed at Eddie with her pinky. "Teach is wearing slacks that aren't at all flexible, not to mention those loafers are pinching his feet. I said six seconds, but he'll be lucky to make it that long."

"Lowest bid wins, then," said Lars, shaking his head with disappointment. He should have considered those factors.

"Captain should have dressed in his cowboy getup like on Gun Barrel," said Knox, who was enjoying himself immensely. Maybe it was the beer mixing with the painkillers, or maybe it was just being around the team.

Lars could relate. His life had significantly improved since joining Ghost Squadron. He missed his family, but now his life had real purpose for what might have been the first time. He had direction.

"If I don't see Teach in a cowboy hat again for the rest of my life it will be too soon," said Julianna, then stood and stretched. In her pants suit she looked dainty, maybe even like an actual vulnerable human, but Lars knew that wasn't at all accurate—appearances were indeed deceiving in her case. "I'm going to get another round. You guys in?"

Both nodded.

When Julianna had left Lars looked at Knox tentatively. There was something he'd been meaning to say since he met the guy, but he didn't really know how. "I'm sorry about your people at Defiance," he finally got out.

Knox swiveled his gaze up to look at Lars, and then away. He touched the side of his glass, then ran his finger through the condensation. "Thanks. I appreciate that."

"I know they were killed by the Brotherhood, and..."

"The Captain said you used to be one of them, but things changed," said Knox after a moment.

"I was *forced* to be one of them. That's what you should have been told. Not all of them are bad. Many are enslaved, like I was," explained Lars.

Knox drew more designs in the condensation on his glass. "Even if I was forced I wouldn't shoot innocent people, not like what they did to the guys and Mateo."

"I agree," said Lars. "I don't think I would either, but it's hard to say what people will do sometimes. The Brotherhood used to tell us that aliens were evil, particularly the Federation. They lied constantly, and those lies mostly worked on the younger generation. I'm old enough to remember when the Kezzin people were better than that. That's why I'm here and not working for the Brotherhood anymore." He took a long, quiet breath. "I work for the universe. However, this silent war isn't black and white, even if we want it to be. People aren't always good or bad. Most of the time we're just gray. Everyone is motivated by different things. Maybe some of those Brotherhood soldiers have families, and if they don't comply then they'll be killed."

Knox pushed out his lips, a thoughtful expression on his face. "Yeah, I guess that's true. It's hard not to hate the people who killed Mateo and Axel, though. I don't think I could ever forgive them, especially Felix Castile."

Lars knew exactly how conflicted emotions confused things. "I know how you feel, but that's why you're here, right? To make a difference, and to stop the Brotherhood and Felix?"

Knox nodded. "Did they kill your family?"

Lars swallowed. He couldn't even fathom such a thing. "No, but they separated us. Pulled me away. All I can think about now is getting back to them and making sure they are all right, but I can't do that yet. I need to know that they will be protected in the future, and that starts with Ghost Squadron."

"You speak with a lot of passion," observed Knox.

Lars almost smiled at this. He'd always thought of himself as simmering with passion, but it had never come out of him until now. "War brings out the best in some, and the worst in others. I'm hoping that all this has made me a better person, not a worse one."

"Seems like it has," said Knox as Julianna returned with four drinks in her hands.

"Looks like it's almost show time," said Julianna, pointing to Eddie. He'd already received the full rundown and signed a waiver. When he held up one hand the crowd around the bull boomed, many of them throwing cowboy hats over their heads.

"Oh, this is going to be good," said Lars, leaning back in his seat and watching eagerly.

Eddie's other hand had been tied tightly to a handle on the saddle. The mechanical bull tilted forward, and he compensated by leaning back.

So far so good, but that's not going to last, thought Julianna.

The bull spun to the side, and then flew backward. Eddie rocked back and forth, clenching his legs to the machine's sides. His shiny loafer slipped just as the bull rocked forward, swerving at the same time. He slid to the side, hand still attached but both legs on one side of the bull, and the contraption picked up intensity, continuing to buck.

Unable to pull himself back up, Eddie finally let go and slid to the mat. The crowd hollered with excitement, many of them urging him to go again. Lying on his back on the mat, Eddie heaved in a breath, his eyes on the ceiling. He got to all fours before pushing to his feet and throwing both hands over his head to encourage the audience.

"All right, moment of truth," said Lars, looking at the screen to the side of the bull that displayed the rider's time.

The screen blinked several times, then two numbers appeared.

5.4

"Yeah!" cheered Julianna.

Knox laughed. "Five and half seconds. You called that one, Commander."

Lars stood up reluctantly, but had a small smile on his face. "All right, you got me this round."

"Time to take your punishment," said Julianna. "Get up there and ride that beast."

He strode toward the bull, and as Eddie passed him he patted Lars on the shoulder. "Hold on tight, there. That bull ain't playin' around."

Buzzing with excitement, Eddie returned to the table and took the seat next to Julianna. "You had me figured, didn't you, Strong Arm?"

"I had your shoes figured, mostly," she said, pointing to the tight leather shoes.

"Ha! Yeah, that's exactly why I got bucked off. Good call," he said, glancing down at them.

Knox had turned around completely and was watching the activity in the bar. He always appeared to look at things with fresh eyes. Julianna guessed he hadn't been in places like this much. Onyx Station hosted things that weren't found anywhere outside Federation space.

"I got us another round," said Julianna, indicating the beer she'd gotten for Eddie.

"Why, thank you kindly, Sally. After a long day at the census bureau, I can't think of anything I want more than a cold beer." Eddie picked up the mug and took a long sip.

Julianna's dropped her eyes as a weird thought occurred to her.

"What's the look for?" asked Eddie, catching the change in her expression.

"I was just thinking how strange it would be to have a normal job like that—one with set hours where you go to the same location," said Julianna. It really seemed as foreign of an idea to her as sleeping in on weekends, or having *actual* weekends. *What day was it, anyway?*

Eddie laughed, then leaned close to her and whispered, "To be honest, it sounds horrible. I don't think people like you and me are well-suited for normal jobs."

"Yeah, there's not much normal about me or my life," said Julianna.

Eddie was still leaning in close, but was now studying Julianna. She pulled back a couple inches to get space.

He tapped his chin as if he were contemplating something. "You ever want that? A normal life? Wish you could have it if you wanted?" asked Eddie.

Julianna picked up her drink, but didn't take a sip. She thought honestly about the questions.

Before she could answer Eddie continued, "You know, a steady job, a family, a mate?"

Julianna threw her head back, emptying her glass. "No. I love my job, and I've never been the family type. Well, unless you count the crew and the squadron."

"And what about a mate? You ever get lonely? Space can be a lonesome place," said Eddie, looking like he was playing a game with her with this questioning.

Julianna shook her head. "The Federation made me who I am and I'll always be grateful for that, but I'm very different from most because of it. No one could ever be right for me, not now that I've changed."

"Because you're enhanced?" asked Eddie.

She paused, but then shrugged. "Something like that."

Eddie nodded, his eyes dropping to his half-drunk beer.

"And to answer your question," said Julianna, "no, I don't get lonely. I don't allow myself the opportunity."

18

Intelligence Center, QBS *ArchAngel*, Paladin System

Eddie rolled his shoulders, glad to be back in his normal clothes. He'd slept fitfully the night before, maybe from being back on Onyx Station, maybe something else. There was a feeling in the back of his head, something he couldn't place.

Julianna and Eddie stood shoulder to shoulder as Jack bustled into the Intelligence Center with a worried expression in his eyes. Jack often looked focused, but rarely did he appear like this. *Anxious*.

When he reached the front of the room Jack cleared his throat, pulling everyone's attention to him. "Thank you for joining me. Some intel came in while you were on Onyx Station. I had Chester look into it, and he's been able to pull quite a bit of information. *Fortunately*, we now know exactly what Felix and the Brotherhood are up to. *Unfortunately*, it's not good at all. I daresay it's worse than I originally envisioned."

Juliana stiffened beside Eddie, her jaw clenching.

Jack gave Chester a brief nod and he dutifully pulled up an image on the main screen. A small blue and green planet with purplish clouds rotated on the monitor.

"Felix has a project in the works, something he's taken to calling "Domination", and it has just one purpose," said Jack, angry heat in his voice. "He's trying to take over a planet."

Julianna tilted her head to the side as if she hadn't heard Jack correctly. "But *why*? What's the purpose of taking that particular planet? I thought he wanted to make the Federation pay for something the General did. How is this related?"

Jack nodded. "That's exactly what he wants, and this is the way he's attempting to do it, utilizing the Brotherhood." Pointing to the screen, Jack flicked his eyes in the direction of the small planet. "This is Nexus. It's a fairly obscure world, but rich in certain resources. Furthermore, the people are at a major disadvantage. From what we can determine the Brotherhood have landed on Nexus and made it their central base of operations, at least for right now. They are enslaving the human natives to serve them. Capable men are being enlisted to fight as grunt soldiers, while others are forced to serve in the local mines."

"And the people are just accepting this?" asked Julianna, disgust in her voice.

"Actually, they aren't," said Jack. "There's now a war on this usually peaceful planet, although I don't expect it to be long before the Brotherhood overpowers them. At that point Felix will have tripled or quite possibly quadrupled his army, and he'll have a powerful home base outside

Federation space. If he succeeds in taking over Nexus, he'll be in a position to attack the Federation."

"How's that?" asked Eddie.

"Nexus isn't far from Federation space, sitting somewhere between the Kezzin and Trid empires," explained Jack. "It's the perfect staging ground for a full-on assault."

"Why hasn't anyone stepped in?" asked Marilla, who was sitting at her desk.

"No one knew what was going on until just recently," explained Jack. "Besides, we believe the local governments in this region have been paid off by Mr. Castile. Were it not for Ghost Squadron's efforts we would not know any of this, not before it was too late."

As Eddie studied the planet's image, a chill ran down his back at the idea that Felix had almost successfully taken over a planet right under their noses.

"You have a mission for us?" asked Julianna.

"Yes. We need to act fast, because Felix has made a fair amount of progress according to the images Chester has found," said Jack. He pointed to the hacker, who sat behind his workstation twirling his pencil.

"When do we go?" asked Eddie.

"You depart at thirteen hundred hours. I'm having ArchAngel send over the details for the mission, so you have just enough time to meet with your team, debrief, and prep," said Jack.

"There's something you're not saying, Jack," said Julianna.

Eddie had sensed that too. It was something in his demeanor. A hesitance, perhaps.

Jack let out a long sigh and threw his hand out. "This

mission—it's exactly why we need to grow this team faster. We need more pilots and we need a ground force, but we don't have all that in place right now. It's going to take time."

"Felix planned this perfectly," said Eddie, seething at the words. "He must know about our team and what we're doing, and he's trying to act before we have time to prepare."

"That he did," said Jack, his tone full of fury. "Since we don't have the numbers we need, we're going to have to rely on strategy. Felix is counting on the Brotherhood to control this region, but that power is centralized in Commander Lytes, not Felix himself. If we take Lytes out, at least, it should dissolve the Brotherhood, but getting in there to do that will be a big problem. There's a war on that planet."

"Could we partner with the natives to increase our numbers?" asked Eddie. "Drop in covertly and start a resistance?"

Jack nodded. "That was the idea. Back on Earth, a ruler named Napoleon would enter his enemy's country and start a civil war before attacking it. It was very efficient." Jack flashed them a cunning smile. "Between this and a few other strategies we'll run simultaneously I think we can get in swiftly and, more importantly, succeed, so long as everything comes together at the end. Just remember, we want Commander Lytes above all else. We need the Brotherhood disbanded."

"You can rely on us, Jack. We will do everything in our power to free the innocent and bring justice to Commander Lytes," said Eddie.

"Good," said Jack, a serious look on his face. "Because if he and Felix are successful in taking over this planet, there won't be anything we can do to stop the war that follows."

Loading Bay 02, QBS *ArchAngel*, Tangki System

A row of modified Black Eagles sat on the front line, each pilot standing at attention. She had only briefly met these new recruits and it pained her, because Jack was right. They were understaffed for this mission, all because they hadn't anticipated what was about to unfold.

Julianna stared at the small fleet, the Eagles barely recognizable with their new design. Hatch had modified them so no one would be able to tell these ships had come from the Federation. In time, of course, their squad would only use Q-Ships, but they had to make do with what they had right now.

Behind the Black Eagles stood the two Q-Ships. Eddie was checking over his Alpha-line model before the mission and Hatch waddled beside him, explaining many of the changes he'd made to the ship to bring it closer to the Omega-line. The Stingray was at the back with Lars in front of it, feet shoulder-width apart and arms rigidly crossed.

"You all have your orders," began Julianna, speaking directly to the pilots. Eddie looked at her with a fierce expression on his face. "This mission isn't going to be easy. Actually, it's fucking complicated, but that shouldn't matter. What matters is that people's freedom is at stake. Some have already been stripped of that natural right. We can't let Felix Castile's influence spread any farther than it already has."

Julianna began to pace, hands behind her back. "No one

knows who we are or why we fight." She halted and stared at the men and women before her, who were all new recruits and all pilots. But they had proved they were hungry for justice, same as Julianna and Eddie. "But you all know what Ghost Squadron's mission is, am I right?"

There was a collective "Yes" from the group, and Lars answered from the back.

"We do what we do because it's worth fighting for," continued Julianna. "We hide on the fringe, punishing those who think they can bully the Federation. The people we are going to help are not a part of the Federation, but their freedoms are at stake or have already been stolen. If we don't fight for them today, they could be *us* tomorrow. We are all at risk of losing the one thing that truly matters. Freedom is not a gift, it is our birth right. I want you to go out there and help us protect the people of Nexus. I want you to help us to disband the Brotherhood, but even after we are successful there will still be more battles to fight. However, we will have defeated one more bully. We will have sent them an important message: The *Federation* may not have been able to stop you, but Ghost Squadron will."

"Nice speech," said Eddie when Julianna met him by the Q-Ships.

"Thanks," she said, acting indifferent.

He'd never seen her quite like that—overcome with passion. It was inspiring, and had been perfectly executed. Concise and powerful. "I didn't know you had that kind of speech in you."

"How do you know I didn't just regurgitate something I've used before?" To his surprise there was a playful smile on her face, although her eyes were serious.

"Did you?" he asked.

She shook her head. "No. Our squadron is about to risk their lives under our command, so they deserve to hear something from the heart."

Eddie smiled, feeling an immense amount of pride. "I agree. *Our* squadron..." It was surreal to think they were in charge of this group, but it felt right.

"You ready to go, Captain?" asked Julianna, looking his ship over.

"You know I am. I was born for this mission, and for the next. And the next," said Eddie, the adrenaline spiking in his blood.

"Be swift. Get in there, and get out. Don't take any unnecessary risks," ordered Julianna, her voice serious.

"Aw, shucks. From the sound of it, Commander, you're worried about me," said Eddie.

"We all have a dangerous mission, but I think we both know you have more at risk," said Julianna, insinuating Eddie's vulnerability.

"Don't worry, Jules, I'll be back on this deck with you by the end of the day, ready to throw back some drinks." Eddie held out his hand to her. "Safe flying, Commander. Watch out for yourself as well. You may be strong, but we all know that no one is invincible."

Julianna eyed his hand before wrapping her fingers around his. They shook briefly, eyes locked. "Will do, Captain."

Eddie climbed aboard his Q-Ship, giving Julianna one last look as she did the same.

When the squadron had departed the loading bay felt strange, and too empty. Hatch eyed the crew, who were working on another Q-Ship. He opened his mouth to tell them they were doing something wrong, but slammed it shut. *What was the point?* It wasn't that the crew was incredibly incompetent. They were actually normal. Average...but that was the problem. Hatch liked to work alone, because he had zero tolerance for "average." He'd never known what it was like to perform typically. Pip kept telling him his expectations were too high, but that wasn't something one changed overnight.

He waddled over to a set of workstations where he was constructing engine parts to be installed in the new Q-Ships.

Someone was already there, he quickly realized. It was the kid with the black Mohawk. Knox, he believed his name was—the boy he had talked to about his car collection.

Knox dropped something on one of the tables and clumsily shuffled backward. "Sorry," he said.

"What are you doing back there?" asked Hatch.

Knox looked up, his face startled. "I was... I just... I saw those parts sitting there... I'm sorry."

Hatch eyed the engine parts on the table. They weren't how he'd left them. He stretched one of his tentacles toward the table and picked up the part, which had been put together...correctly.

"Did you do this?" asked Hatch, narrowing his eyes at the kid.

"I'm sorry. Yes. I was just messing around, and before I knew it I had done this. I apologize if I messed it up. Please let me fix it," said Knox, his voice frantic.

"Fix it? How can you fix *that*?" asked Hatch, his tone still brooding.

"I can take it back apart." Knox hobbled behind the table again, still seeming really clumsy—like he was hopping. "Please, I'll do whatever you say! Just don't tell the Commander or the Captain I messed up your parts. They'll kick me out. They'll make me leave."

Hatch regarded the turbo pump in his tentacle, trying to hide anything that might be in his expression. "You think they'll kick you off the team?"

Knox nodded. "I'm still new, and on a trial basis. I'm really sorry. I don't know why I messed with your engine parts, it's just, they *called* to me. I should know better."

"You should *definitely* know better," said Hatch, turning the connected pieces over in his tentacle to inspect them. "These parts called to you, you say?" The form wasn't standard. It was clear this boy had never assembled a piece like this before but he'd found a way to do it, making it just as efficient as if Hatch had done it himself. For someone with no experience, this was impressive. "Who showed you how to do this?" Hatch asked him.

The boy shook his head. "No one did. It was like a blueprint appeared in my head. Something makes me think I know how to put things together. I know it's dumb. I don't even have any formal schooling," said Knox, "not like the people on your crew. My old boss Mateo taught me how to fix my ship, so I guess you could say that was how I learned the basics."

"You're right. My crew all has engineering degrees, although most of them have more credentials after their name than brain cells in their heads," said Hatch.

"Oh, right. Well, I won't touch your stuff anymore. I won't even come down here again. And if you want me to, I'll fix what I've done," said Knox.

"Fix? There's nothing to fix," said Hatch, laying the turbo pump back down on the workstation.

"Wait, there isn't? What are you saying?" asked Knox, his eyes wide.

He was just a kid, but there was something perfect about the young. They hadn't been corrupted by other people's practices or taught the wrong way to do things at some stuffy school. They hadn't been taught to trust text-book practices over intuition and gut instinct, which was why Hatch had patented so many inventions. For a lack of a better phrase, he thought outside the box. Hell, he *lived* outside the box, as far as his thinking went.

"I'm saying that you constructed this turbo pump correctly. Not only that, but you connected them perfectly. Usually a newbie...or a member of my worthless crew," Hatch yelled loudly enough for the crew shuffling around behind him to hear, "fits the bearing on too tightly or cross-threads it."

"Oh, well... Rookie luck, I guess," said Knox, his face flushing red.

"I've never met a rookie who could put together a turbo

pump correctly on his first try without blueprints," said Hatch.

Knox shrugged. "I dunno, I see connections in my head when it comes to mechanics. That's how I was able to fix *Catfish.*"

"Yeah, I had a chance to look at that Black Eagle you fixed up," said Hatch. "The control drum needs to be repaired."

Knox nodded. "Yeah, I know. I checked my girl this morning. I haven't gotten around to the control drum, and the internal shield is mostly shot, but none of that is worth fixing if I can't get the propellant line clear. The engine took serious damage on my trip here."

It was astonishing that this kid knew all that. He covered his surprise with a scowl, though. Hatch turned his head to the side, regarding Knox with one eye and the crew with the other. "What are you doing here anyway?" he asked. "You can pilot. Why didn't you go on the mission?"

Knox reached to the ground and retrieved two crutches, then positioned them under his armpits and hobbled around the table. Once he was in clear view, Hatch noticed a cast on one of his feet. "I broke my foot when I was at Onyx Station, and I've been decommissioned for the moment. Not even sure what purpose Ghost Squadron will have for me now. I'm pretty useless."

"Feet mend, especially with the Federation technology we can get," said Hatch.

"Yeah, that was what the Captain said. He's working on getting a regeneration pill for me. It's just that this mission today is really important. This Commander Lytes, he's one of the people responsible for what happened to my old crew." He lowered his eyes. "I wanted to go with everyone, be a part of the efforts to bring him down, but I'm stuck here doing nothing."

"Pilots are definitely at the heart of attacks that stop people like Commander Lytes," began Hatch, holding up one tentacle for silence. "However, a pilot is worthless without a ship, and we currently have more pilots than we do ships to fly."

Knox leaned on one of his crutches, putting most of his weight on his good foot. "Yeah, you're right. Even if I *could* fly, I probably wasn't going to be able to join today. I'm not even formally trained."

"That wasn't what I was saying," corrected Hatch.

Knox blinked at him, confusion evident in his gaze. "You weren't? What'd you mean?"

"I meant that having pilots is important, but they are useless without mechanics to construct the ships and keep them maintained," started Hatch. "What Ghost Squadron needs more than newbie pilots is a mechanic who shows promise, one who can see the inner workings of an engine using an intuitive perspective. One who can assemble a turbo pump from instinct."

Knox's mouth dropped open and his eyes widened. He nearly toppled over on the crutch he was leaning on. "You mean me? You think I... Even after..."

Hatch cleared his throat. "I think you show more promise than any of the hundreds of applicants I've interviewed. I've hired the best, but none of them display a natural talent for mechanics like you do, because it's rare. Most are *taught* how things work. Few naturally understand it."

If Hatch was honest with himself, there was only one other who he knew who had a natural instinct for mechanics. And he knew that Londil well—better than anyone.

"Are you offering me a spot on your crew?" asked Knox.

Hatch looked over his shoulder at the crew, who were tirelessly trying to please his impossible expectations. "No. My crew is full."

"Oh, I misunderstood," said Knox.

"And besides, if you were to work with those dimwits you'd learn bad practices, ones that I can't unteach *them* because they've been drilled in by formal schooling," said Hatch.

"What exactly are you offering me?" asked Knox.

"A position as my apprentice, if you're interested. You would only work with me. The things you would learn would come from only me. No bad practices would be forced on you," said Hatch.

"Are you serious? You're the very best, though, and I'm a nobody—"

"I'm a mechanic who needs an apprentice. The job will be demanding, and you'll constantly be tested. I'm not going to try and convince you. All I'll say is, you're a good fit. If you want the position, just say it," said Hatch, twining his tentacles across his chest.

Knox shook his head as if to rid it of cobwebs. The kid was completely dazed by this changing of events. For a human, his newness was kind of endearing.

After a long moment Hatch sighed impatiently. "Well, I guess you're not ready. Maybe you aren't—"

"I'll do it!" yelled Knox, gaining the attention of many of

the crew in the distance. "I'll do it," he said a bit more quietly.

Hatch nodded. "Good choice, Gunner. Your first job is to go to Sick Bay and get a regeneration pill."

"What? No, the Captain said they didn't have any..."

"Of course they do. This is the *ArchAngel*," explained Hatch, puffing his cheeks out. "They're just holding them in case of emergency. You go down there and tell them I sent you. They'll get you taken care of, because if they don't they'll have to deal with *me*. And trust me, kid, no one wants that."

19

Omega-line Q-Ship, Nexus, Tangki System

Julianna landed the Q-Ship in the area Chester had identified as friendly Nexus territory. He'd also been able to send correspondence to the people, explaining who they were and their intention. These were primitive people, mostly living in huts and tents, but there was something sophisticated about how they used the resources and didn't deplete them. That was one reason that Nexus was so rich in minerals and other useful resources.

Chester had encoded a video message from Julianna in a small capsule that they'd dropped on Nexus-occupied territory. It carried a blinking yellow light, which according to the research Marilla had done on these humans was synonymous with "friendly."

In addition to the video message, a light projector had been included. It was small, but when pressed it sent up a beam of light that could penetrate orbit—a cleverly-designed invention of Hatch's. The end of Julianna's video message had been simple: "If you want our help over-throwing the Brotherhood, click the light projector twice. If you do not want our help, click it once. But be warned: the Brotherhood is under the influence of a dangerous man who will use your planet and your people and dispose of them once he's taken everything you hold dear."

An hour after the capsule landed, the *ArchAngel* recorded two light beams projected from the western continent of Nexus. They were on-planet now, ready to partner with strangers to fight a larger evil. It continued to amaze Julianna how those so separate and different could bond together to fight a common enemy. No one was really isolated when they had a mutual goal.

The small planet of Nexus was diverse, with lush lands full of mineral-rich caves and an underground stocked with oil and other natural resources. The waters that bordered the land were a pristine blue, the coral reefs full of vegetation and exotic animal life. Julianna hadn't seen a planet like this...well, for too long. Most of the planets she'd visited were dominated by a single type of terrain, or boasted only one climate. Not Nexus...it had the right balance of land and water, mountains and plains. Its vege-tation and population suggested the climate had a proper spectrum and that the year would be marked by four distinct seasons.

Julianna squinted against the bright sun overhead. She held her hand up to cover her eyes and looked at the area before her, which was full of huts and tall trees. Stepping forward, she lowered her hand so the group in the distance could see her face clearly.

A human woman with long blonde hair braided into

four sections stepped toward her. She was incredibly beautiful, as were all the people behind her, who all had light hair and tanned skin. Most, like the leader, wore long and flowing white robes. As she approached, Julianna noted the feathers the men had braided into their hair, and the beautifully detailed beaded necklaces and bracelets the women wore.

"I am Alleira, the leader of this continent, which is called 'Sunex,'" the woman said, spreading her arms wide to indicate the land where they stood. "You're the one who sent the message?"

"Yes. I'm Julianna, the Commander of Ghost Squadron. We're here to assist you and protect you, and help you protect yourself," said Julianna.

A pained look crossed the woman's face, suddenly making her appear much older than she was. "These savages have taken over the eastern half of Sunex, causing our people to retreat." She pointed to the horizon, which arched oddly due to the planet's small size.

"Our surveillance shows they are moving in this direction," said Julianna.

The woman nodded solemnly. "Yes. They have a foothold on our eastern shores now, and we've been told to surrender or fight. They've promised that by nightfall there will be no other option for my people."

"There's always another option." Julianna regarded the beautiful landscape around her before returning her gaze to Alleira. "War creates destruction, which takes a long time to recover from. Although I can't promise there will be no damage, my team has a strategy that we think will preserve your planet."

"We've asked the gods for a solution that suited our long-term growth rather than just saving us." Alleira smiled, the expression transforming her face into something breathtaking. "I see that the gods answered our prayers with you."

Julianna offered her own smile, hers much subtler. "I have devices in my ship, and I need every able body to place them. I'll explain exactly how it works once we get started. Is that all right?"

Alleira looked at her council, each of whom nodded curtly, and turned back. "Commander, we will follow your lead. Our future is in your hands."

Stingray, Nexus, Tangki System

The controls of the Stingray were just different enough that Lars had to check himself often as he flew the ship through the atmosphere of Nexus. It felt strange to wear his old Brotherhood uniform, but it was for a good purpose, so he didn't mind. It didn't give the Kezzin the same constricted feeling as it used to.

"What's your status, Carnivore?" asked Eddie over the comm.

Lars leveled the controls as he fell in with a squad of Stingrays. His chest tightened as enemy ships flew around him, each occupied by a Brotherhood soldier.

"I'm in formation, headed to the main base," said Lars.

"Very good." Eddie sighed loudly. "I'm in position, and await your intel."

Lars let out his own heavy breath. It was hard for him to fathom that the Captain was sitting inconspicuously in the airspace over the Brotherhood's base, Q-Ship cloaked as he waited to find out Commander Lytes' location. As long as the Brotherhood didn't suspect anything they wouldn't turn on the sensor which would detect the Q-Ship, which was why Lars had to stay undercover.

"Landing now on the eastern side of the base," said Lars, looking out at the blue ocean in the distance. It was a beautiful location, just not for an enemy base.

"Copy that, Carnivore," said Eddie. "Be careful and stay in contact."

Lars directed the ship to the ground, taking commands from the crew who stood on the tarmac and waved each ship into a line. The dozens and dozens of Stingrays sat in rows. The Brotherhood definitely had the numbers, which meant the strategy had to be perfect if they were going to stop them. If Julianna didn't pull off her end they'd be overwhelmed easily, and just as importantly, Eddie had to cut off the head of the Brotherhood beast.

Copying the Brotherhood soldier who had parked next to him, Lars exited his Stingray and marched into line, following the long stretch of soldiers as they formed up. His breath caught at the sea of Brotherhood males, both Trid and Kezzin, but mostly the latter. The army's numbers had exploded since he'd been a part of it.

The only good thing about the size of the army was that no one would recognize Lars and know he was the traitor who had helped Julianna and Eddie escape in the past. Once at the back of the formation, Lars released a breath he hadn't even realized he had been holding.

Now the real challenges began. The first was to find the Commander's location, which would be inside the main base in a protected room. *Protected but still penetrable,* he thought. After that, Lars had to get out of there before he was sent into combat. Above all, he couldn't be caught. The Brotherhood would not allow him to survive if they found out who he was and who he worked for.

Eddie drummed his fingers on the controls as he watched the Brotherhood base from the air.

"Are you nervous?" asked Pip from the overhead speaker.

"No, just restless," answered Eddie.

"You're nervous, based on the twitch on the left side of your face, dilated pupils, and fidgeting."

"Do you do this sort of thing to Julianna?" asked Eddie.

"She likes it," joked Pip.

"How is Jules doing?" asked Eddie.

"*Jules* is making progress with the natives," said Pip, emphasis on Eddie's nickname for Julianna. "They are setting the mock mines as we speak."

Eddie drummed his fingers absently. "I really hope this works."

"Is that what the Captain depends on when all preparations have been made and execution is all that's left? Hope?"

"Hope is always a part of the equation, no matter what stage we're in," said Eddie.

He peered down at the base the Brotherhood had constructed seemingly overnight, which was comprised largely of temporary buildings and tents. It was hard to tell where the Command Center was located, and that was what Lars had to figure out. There would no doubt be traps, since Commander Lytes would know that Ghost Squadron had been on a hunt for information when he was discovered at Pistris Station. However, he was wrong if he thought they'd attack the Brotherhood base. That wasn't going to happen with Lars on the ground. Only two people should pay for what the Brotherhood were doing.

After a long speech had been delivered by Commander Lytes over speakers around the base, the soldiers were dismissed. Lars started forward with his line, and the males marched back to their ships, their orders having been given. He wanted to find it hard to believe that they had been instructed to shoot at the people of Sunex on this continent to force them back, but Lars knew better. The Brotherhood were often ordered to do despicable things, all for a stronger power which every one of them believed owned him.

When the people of Sunex retreated they'd be surrounded and taken prisoner, and then the whole scenario would take place again and again until the planet had been subjugated by the Brotherhood. Or at least that was the plan Commander Lytes communicated to the soldiers, telling them this was a part of their destiny, and that their loyalty would be rewarded and their insolence punished.

Lars sped past the Stingray he'd flown in on. He had no

plans to fly off in formation and follow Commander Lytes' orders.

He hurried by a set of barracks, which was what he realized they were after peeking into the first building. The structures all looked alike, which he was certain had been done on purpose.

"Soldier, what are you doing?" a Brotherhood lieutenant asked, causing Lars to halt.

He straightened and saluted. "I was given orders to relay a message to the Commander, sir."

"By whom?" asked the lieutenant. His forehead had wrinkled in skepticism.

Lars didn't hesitate. "By the technical sergeant, sir."

The male narrowed his eyes. "By *who?*" he repeated.

"By the tech—"

"What is his *name*, Private?" the lieutenant boomed.

Lars' hand rose above his gun, but only slightly. "I was told to alert the Commander to a problem with the Stingray fleet."

"Why wouldn't this have been sent over the radio to the Command Center?" asked the lieutenant.

Lars hesitated now, choking on his next words.

The lieutenant's face turned a shade darker, and with less stealth than Lars he reached for his weapon, at which Lars yanked his pistol out of his holster and shot the male in the head. The lieutenant landed hard on his back with a shocked expression on his newly modified face.

"Are you all right?" asked Eddie on the comm.

Lars stared down at the body. "Yes. I...had to defend myself."

There was a sigh in his ear from the other end of the channel. "Okay, be careful. Good work covering for us."

Lars allowed himself a brief moment to press his eyes shut and ask for silent forgiveness for what he'd been forced to do, but his eyes sprang open a second later. He grabbed the male's shoulder and dragged him between two buildings. The gunfire shouldn't have been heard over the noise from the Stingrays taking flight, but might still have attracted attention.

Once the male's body had been hidden from view, Lars slipped back out from between the buildings and sprinted forward, ducking into each building he came to. At this point time was the most crucial factor. The siege would start soon, and the Commander would know that Ghost Squadron had intervened.

Three males filed out of a building ahead, so Lars ducked into a shadow of a vehicle and crouched close to the ground. He tried his best to read the rank insignia on each of their uniforms from between the tires, which would tell him enough to make a useful assumption.

"Do you believe what the Commander just said?" asked one of the males as they charged by. Soon they'd be out of earshot, and also too far away for Lars to read their ranks.

"That after this we'll be ready to attack the Federation? Yeah, it's hard to believe," said one of the other males. They continued to talk as they moved and their voices grew indistinct. Lars' gaze fell on the building they'd just come out of.

"Blackbeard, I've found our target," he whispered.

Eddie landed the cloaked Q-Ship next to the building Lars had indicated, and he raised the tri-rifle before opening the hatch.

"Tell Jules I'm going in," said Eddie to Pip.

There was a long moment of silence before a sigh came from overhead. "She said good luck, but that wasn't what she meant," said Pip.

Eddie chuckled. "What did she mean?"

"Don't die," said Pip morbidly.

"Tell her not to worry. I'm bringing the big guns, and soon we'll have Lytes sitting across the table in the interrogation room spilling all his secrets."

After another pause Pip responded, "Julianna says she's not worried."

"Oh, well, that's good," said Eddie.

"But Captain…" said Pip.

Eddie paused before disembarking. "Yes?"

"Just between you and me, she is."

"It must mean she cares," said Eddie.

"She says it's because training your replacement would be a bitch," said Pip.

"Tell her not to fret. I can be replaced *easily*," said Eddie.

"Actually, you should know that General Reynolds picked you because of the incident in the Lorialis System. It wouldn't be easy to find someone else who could have accomplished that," said Pip.

"I didn't do anything any other leader wouldn't have done," said Eddie, recalling the long-ago affair like it had been yesterday. It wasn't hard to remember, since it was often a part of a reoccurring dream.

"Leaders are taught not to leave a man behind, but

many do. They often say they are protecting the team, protecting the greater good. Few live up to that motto in battle, and most don't go back to save soldiers considered doomed," said Pip.

"I made a promise to those men that I would sooner die than leave them behind," said Eddie through gritted teeth. Pip was getting bolder, and he could understand why Julianna didn't always appreciate it.

"And you did almost die to save the two men," said Pip.

"Numbers aren't really important. A person is a person, and each means something to someone," said Eddie.

"All I'm trying to say is that the General picked you for a reason, one not many other people can claim. You're a man who does what he says he'll do, even if you have to risk your life to keep your word. Julianna might joke, but she'd have trouble replacing you."

"Yeah, I'd like to think you're right," said Eddie.

"It would take at least one, maybe two or three hours to find someone," joked Pip.

"Ha. Ha. You're priceless." Eddie stepped out of the Q-Ship, and the bright sun made him squint slightly.

"Good luck, Captain Teach," said Pip.

"Thanks, Pip."

Soundlessly the hatch closed behind Eddie.

20

Nexus, Tangki System

Julianna gazed at the lush green hills in the distance. Soon the Brotherhood would charge over the ridge to take the land behind her and its people.

Well, they'll try, she thought.

She turned to Alleira, whose forehead glistened with sweat. The people of Sunex had worked hard for the last few hours, and this leader now held the remote switch Hatch had created.

"You know what to do, right?" asked Julianna.

With a fierce look in her eyes, Alleira nodded. "What if it doesn't work?"

"It will work," Julianna assured her.

"I appreciate your enthusiasm, Warrior of the Stars, but even the wisest of our gods consider failure as an option."

Julianna drew in a breath. She couldn't tell Alleira that they were doomed if this strategy didn't work. That the Brotherhood had enough numbers to take them all out. A commander didn't lie, but they could choose which truths to tell. Courage in battle was more important than the weapons one held, and that proceeded from confidence.

Pointing to the clear blue sky, Julianna said, "If all else fails, look to the sky. That's where you'll find hope."

Alleira nodded, her chiseled jaw strong. "Thank you, Commander Fregin. My people have never cared what happens out in space, but we're grateful that there are protectors like you to help us."

Julianna offered one last smile before turning for her Q-Ship.

Brotherhood Headquarters, Nexus, Tangki System

Eddie spotted Lars in the exact location he said he'd be. The Kezzin had a weighted look in his eyes from the kill. Even in battle, when death was expected, the experience stayed with the person, and this was one of Lars' former people, a Brotherhood soldier. Funny that they called it "the Brotherhood" when nothing could be farther from the truth.

"You know the plan," stated Eddie.

Lars nodded abruptly.

"Once you've completed your part, communicate the message to the Brotherhood," said Eddie.

"Will do," said Lars, his voice scratchy.

Eddie raised the heavy tri-rifle and a new focus spread through his mind as he led the way to the building they now knew was the Command Center. Gravel crunched under his boots, but in the middle of the base there was no one out. They were with the Stingrays, or readying to march forward. It didn't matter, though. Wherever each Brotherhood soldier was, he'd get the message when the time came.

Eddie cast a tentative look over his shoulder at Lars, an expression that asked, "Are you ready to kick some ass?"

Lars rolled his shoulders back and this time nodded with true conviction.

Eddie thrust his foot into the door caving it in, but it didn't break.

"I was kind of expecting that they had locked and reinforced it. Actually, I was hoping they had." He set the tri-rifle to demolition mode. "Stand back," he said to Lars, who complied immediately.

Eddie pulled the trigger and a large blast shot horizontally from the gun, tearing the door off and destroying the wall around it. He didn't wait for the smoke and dust to clear, since that was what the forces inside would do. Instead he bolted forward, turning the controls on the tri-rifle to the "spray and stun" option.

Over a dozen Brotherhood soldiers stood at the ready, many squinting from the dust. The Command Center was lined with monitors and computer stations, and in the middle stood Commander Lytes, his beady eyes narrowed on Eddie. Before he could spout a command Eddie fired the tri-rifle at the closest cluster of soldiers, and they dropped instantly, stunned. They appeared to be statues on the ground, stiff and motionless.

"Surrender now! We have the building surrounded," lied Eddie. Lars took his position at the Captain's side, rifle at the ready and aimed at the Commander.

He stood in front of a large console. On the screen was

a digital map, and around it were several red buttons. "You've made a big mistake by coming here," said Commander Lytes, his mouth puckering like he'd just eaten something sour.

"You made a mistake by thinking that you could take over this planet," said Eddie as he scanned the room. All the soldiers except for Lytes still had their guns pointed at Eddie and Lars.

"It's too late," said Lytes. "This world is already ours."

"We disagree, so lower your weapons," said Eddie.

The Brotherhood soldiers stayed put, guns directed at the two. Eddie swiveled the tri-rifle to the set on the other side of the room and fired once, the laser stunning three of the soldiers. They fell to the ground, frozen.

"Drop your weapons," commanded Eddie, his voice loud and clear.

The soldiers in the room all lowered their weapons to the ground, and then their hands went up.

"No, you morons! They're bluffing," cried Lytes.

"We're not. This base has been surrounded by our forces. It's too late for you," said Eddie.

Lytes slammed his fist on the console in front of him. "That's impossible!"

"Ground forces in place," a voice crackled overhead. It was a field officer, ready to lead the troops into battle. "Marching on enemy in five."

Eddie swallowed hard, but his expression was full of confidence. "I assure you it's very possible," said Eddie, swiveling the tri-rifle to cover the various males stationed around the room. "Now, you gentlemen are going to go with Lieutenant Malseen here, where you will meet our other forces. Don't try anything, or he will be forced to shoot. *Am I clear?*"

"Stingrays in position," said a different voice on the radio.

The males muttered their consent, filing into a line and heading for the exit. After Lars followed the last one out, Eddie turned his full attention to Commander Lytes. Everything had gone to plan so far, but it was going to go to shit unless the commander truly believed they were losing. *Come on, Julianna. It's your turn,* Eddie said to himself.

Omega-line Q-Ship, Nexus, Tangki System

Julianna hovered the Q-Ship over the eastern hills. She could clearly see the Brotherhood's base just off the coast, their forces in formation and marching inland right on schedule. The Stingrays lifted off the ground one after the other.

Julianna's pulse sped up as the Brotherhood started their attack.

To the west, the people of Sunex were gathered in their village. Alleira would be on the front line with the switch-box in her hands, and her people had been instructed to retreat if the Brotherhood made it down the hill. There were things worth dying for, but not today. These people needed to resist, but they shouldn't have to make the ultimate sacrifice—not when they were fighting an army of slaves. Commander Lytes and Felix Castile were the ones who needed to pay for these injustices.

"Strong Arm to Ghost Squadron. Hold formation.

Brotherhood ground forces are on the move. Air forces are circling above," said Julianna over the comm to her team.

Her ship was cloaked, allowing her a closer position than the Black Eagles, which were stationed just high enough in the atmosphere to be out of sight. It was crucial that the Brotherhood not know there were outside forces aiding the Sunex people. That would ensure their guard was down, and thus the first attack would be even more startling. The Brotherhood thought they were marching on a defenseless and peaceful people who made pottery and tapestries rather than bombs. The greater their surprise, the stronger the message to Commander Lytes.

Your blood pressure is rising, said Pip in Julianna's head.

Shocking, she replied.

Aerial footage shows Lieutenant Malseen leading six Brotherhood soldiers from a building I would guess is the Command Center.

Okay, right on schedule. Now we just need to offer Teach a confidence boost.

Julianna watched as the long row of Brotherhood soldiers hiked up the hill, carrying their weapons at the ready. They were quickly approaching the first line of mines they'd set up, and when they were fifteen feet from the barrier Julianna held her breath.

Do it, Alleira, she thought to herself.

Nothing happened. The Brotherhood advanced, crossed the top of the ridge, and began making their descent.

Now! Come on, Alleira!

Julianna had placed the controls in the hands of the

leader of the Sunex people, which had seemed like the right thing to do. This was *her* land to defend, after all.

The Brotherhood forces moved as one, now only a few feet from the first line of defense. If they got there first, the ruse might be compromised.

Now! Now! Now! Do it! thought Julianna.

An explosion bloomed from the ground, sending large plumes of gray smoke into the air. The Brotherhood's formation broke, the males halting before backing up. Some ran forward, but there was another explosion. And another. And another.

"Yes! The first mock mines have detonated," said Julianna over the comm.

A chorus of cheers answered her.

"That's great, Strong Arm," came a pilot's voice.

Lone Wolf, Julianna thought, instantly placing one of the newest recruits.

The Brotherhood soldiers had scattered now, and many of them were falling back. Some had been scared enough to run forward, afraid the blast was behind them as well. That was a benefit of setting up the mines on the mountain —it was hard to see where the explosions were coming from.

Another round of explosions rocked the area between the Brotherhood and the Sunex people—and from the sky the explosions appeared lethal, so from the ground they were probably terrifying. However, fireworks could also look quite intimidating if one didn't know they were meant for mostly show and harmless from a distance. That had been the plan—to make it look as though the Brother-hood were under fire by treacherous bombs when in fact the bombs were all blanks, meant to scare and cause a retreat.

Julianna pressed her lips together. *So far, so good.*

Brotherhood Command Center, Nexus, Tangki System

"Sir, we're under heavy fire here!" a voice called over the radio.

Commander Lytes' eyes fell on the radio, his expression confused.

"There are bombs everywhere, and many soldiers are down," came the voice again.

"I told you that we had you surrounded. You've lost this war, Commander," said Eddie, hiking up the tri-rifle in his hands.

Commander Lytes' hand twitched by his side and he tried to reach for the radio, but a single shake of Eddie's head stopped him.

"You will send a message over that radio in just a minute, but you're going to say exactly what I tell you to," said Eddie.

"I don't have to do a damn thing you tell me," snarled Commander Lytes.

Eddie nodded at the tri-rifle and then at the many soldiers still on the ground. "I'm afraid you do. Now, either do everything I say and your soldiers will watch you walk out of here…or you can disobey and they will watch you be dragged out. The one thing that is certain is that your people *will* see you leave here. The only way to free the Brotherhood is if they know you're *gone.*"

The commander's sharp teeth were bared as he hissed

at Eddie, "I do not take orders from you. I'm in charge here!"

"The perimeter is completely blocked. There's no way in or out from on the ground," said a voice over the radio.

"It appears you're *not* in charge anymore," said Eddie, a satisfied grin on his face.

"No response from Commander Lytes," said a different voice over the radio.

Eddie and Lytes eyed the radio, both eager to hear what would come across it next.

"Sending in Stingrays now. Tell the ground forces to retreat," said a new voice on the wire.

Lars followed the six Brotherhood soldiers back to the main area where they'd lined up before. It was fairly empty now, almost all of the forces having been sent into the field and the Stingrays into the air.

The males who remained on the field looked up, questions and bewilderment on their faces at the sight of Brotherhood soldiers with their hands raised.

Lars surprised himself when his voice shot from his mouth. "Ghost Squadron has the base surrounded. You will not be harmed, but you must stand down. Commander Lytes has been taken into custody. This fight is over."

There was a great rustling from the soldiers surrounding the area, and sweat trickled into Lars' eyes. There was only one of him and dozens of them, but Eddie's earlier words from their brief private moment came back to him, seeming extra-important now: *This is a show of intimidation, that is all. The person who says he has the biggest stick will win, whether he actually has it or not."*

Lars aimed his gun at the row of soldiers in front of him. "All of you will be freed, but you must first surrender. Ghost Squadron doesn't want to hurt you."

"How do we know you've taken over our base?" asked one of the six males who had been led from the Command Center.

That was an excellent question, thought Lars, looking at the sky.

Omega-line Q-Ship, Nexus, Tangki System

Mock bombs exploded and the dust got closer to the border of Sunex as some of the Brotherhood soldiers attempted to move around the explosions. Most had retreated, but many were still trying to snake themselves through, fighting for a hold.

A neat formation of Stingray ships darted down from their holding position.

"Party time!" said Julianna. "Ghost Squadron, we have approaching enemy ships. Get them to follow you out to sea. I don't want any ships going down over land. I made a promise to the leader, Alleira."

"You got it, Commander," said several voices over the comm.

"Lone Wolf and Escrima, I want you two down at the base to provide cover for Carnivore. Something tells me he's going to need it," said Julianna, holding her position in the sky. She would drop into battle if needed, but right now she had to watch the action and make the calls. That was the best thing, since Eddie was on the ground going after Commander Lytes.

Julianna watched as the Black Eagles swooped down and barreled toward the approaching Stingrays. The enemy ships shot at her pilots, but all of them missed the fast moving vehicles. Her crew teased the Stingrays, getting their attention— which was exactly what they wanted. The squadron flew over their heads and toward the sea to get the Brotherhood craft to follow them. With no ships flying this way the forces on the ground were defenseless, harassed by bomb after bomb. However, soon someone would realize that the bombs were fake, and then the people of Sunex would be in real trouble.

Julianna watched nervously, her hands tight on the controls of the Q-Ship. If it came to real trouble, she'd aid Alleira. It would involve destroying the land, but desperate times called for firepower action.

Brotherhood Base, Nexus, Tangki System

Two Black Eagles dropped and hovered at Lars' back. He pivoted his head just enough to make out their forms.

Right on time, he thought, *and with not a moment to spare.*

The males he held at gunpoint were growing anxious, many with shifty looks in their eyes. Now all of them straightened, many raising their hands to the sky in surrender. It was hard not to comply when one stared at the cannons tacked to the hovering Black Eagles.

"As I was saying, you've been relieved of your orders. Your commander is now in our custody, and all of you are under our protection." Lars cleared his throat, a strange new buzzing taking over his chest. "You are free from your duty to the Brotherhood, and free to return to Kezza."

No one cheered or even moved, but the change of expression on everyone's faces was palpable. It was like a great weight had fallen off the shoulders of every male in the general vicinity.

This is going to work, thought Lars. They just needed the last step in the plan to fall into place. Commander Lytes had to be marched into custody.

The Q-Ship Eddie had cloaked and parked next to the Command Center lifted into the air, a solid form. It hovered there for a moment before landing on the open patch of tarmac that had been occupied by hundreds of Brotherhood soldiers earlier.

The soldiers held at gunpoint by Lars and the Black Eagles turned to watch the Q-Ship. They were waiting for someone to come out of it, not realizing it had been steered by an AI. No one *would* exit the ship, its sole purpose being to take Commander Lytes away.

Omega-line Q-Ship, Nexus, Tangki System

Julianna watched from the air as the Q-Ship rose above the Brotherhood base, then dropped again. Everything was now in place.

Yes, the Brotherhood forces were gaining on the Sunex people, but there weren't many of them, and soon they'd be called back. The Stingrays were far out to sea chasing the Black Eagles.

Once they had Commander Lytes in custody they'd learn everything they needed to about Felix Castile. Best of all, he'd have lost his footing with the Brotherhood and relinquished his claim to Nexus. Felix would be in an incredibly compromised position.

Next on their list was to find the armory of weapons Felix stole from the Defiance Trading Company. That would all happen, though, in good time.

Brotherhood Command Center, Nexus, Tangki System

"Ground forces have been overrun by bombs. We're pulling back!" yelled a voice over the radio.

Commander Lytes' eyes narrowed in disdain and he ground his fist into the top of the console.

"This is Flight Control Center. It appears that Brotherhood forces from Base Center have been detained," said a robotic voice over the radio.

Commander Lytes' gaze shifted back and forth as the different voices spilled over the radio, all of them frantic.

"Air forces taking enemy fire over the water. About to submerge to reconvene and throw off their attacks," said a different voice.

Eddie smiled inwardly. They'd planned on the Stingrays using their swim technology, which was exactly why they had been led out over the water. The Stingrays had all sped in that direction, thinking they had the advantage and not realizing they were being led away from the Sunex people. By the time they'd pulled off their fancy underwater synchronization act it would all be over. The Brotherhood would have fully surrendered.

"It's too late, like I said before." Eddie held the tri-rifle up, making sure that Commander Lytes didn't forget that this weapon was still in play in the negotiation.

"What do you want from me?" asked the commander, his voice stressed.

"First I want you to pick up the radio on my command and inform all units that this is finished. Pull back ground and air forces, recalling them to the base. Tell them your command has been overthrown," said Eddie.

"And then what?" growled Lytes.

Eddie smiled, feeling the adrenaline start to wane as the imminent success became reality. "And then we're going to take a little walk, just the two of us." He motioned with the gun to the exit. "You're going to march out in front of your army in handcuffs and board my ship. You won't be harmed, but from now until your trial you will be a prisoner of the Federation."

The commander ground his sharp teeth, a screeching noise coming from his mouth with the movement. "Felix won't let you get away with this."

"Felix isn't here," said Eddie with a deep laugh. "Your great and powerful master has left you all alone. He told you to take this planet, but where is he when someone tries to stop you? He wanted you to do his dirty work, then he'd swoop in when everything was safe. Well, imagine his surprise when he learns you've failed and you're our little prisoner! I can just see the look in his eyes."

"You underestimate Mr. Castile," said the commander.

Eddie tilted his head to the side. "Do I? You're the one taking orders from me, so I don't think I do. Now, pick up the radio and announce your defeat. If you try anything funny I'll shoot you, and then you'll be dragged out of here in a very undignified manner. And let's be honest, Lytes—all you have left is your dignity, am I right?"

The commander snatched up the radio, his eyes two tiny slits, then took a deep breath and opened his mouth.

Brotherhood Base, Nexus, Tangki System

Static filled the speakers around the base and then a voice Lars recognized immediately came through. *Lytes.*

Everyone tensed as they listened to the message.

"This is Commander Lytes of the Brotherhood. Our base has been overrun by the enemy. Our ground forces are down, and our ships are in compromised territory. I have..." there was a pause, and the commander cleared his throat. "It is with regret that I must inform you we have surrendered to enemy forces. I ask that you all stand down. Return to base, and relinquish control to Ghost Squadron. I repeat: ground forces, return to the base. Air forces, do not submerge, return to base. We have been overrun by the enemy."

Lars' hands tightened on his gun as the Brotherhood soldiers before him turned to each other in astonishment. Oh, they'd believed him when the Black Eagles had hovered, reinforcing him, but now reality was setting in. Most had anxious faces, but underneath that Lars thought he recognized another emotion: relief. Every single one of these soldiers knew that this was now someone else's war, that it was over for them. That the Brotherhood was being disbanded meant something of great value: They would be free to return home.

Brotherhood Command Center, Nexus, Tangki System

Eddie waited until Commander Lytes had finished his address and placed the radio transmitter on the console before nodding his approval.

"Nicely done," he said. "You know, for a despicable male who abuses his power, you still have some honor left in you."

"Your idea of honor and mine are very different," hissed Lytes.

Eddie shrugged, enjoying the Kezzin's display of anger more than he should have.

"You say 'pot-ay-to,' I say 'pot-ah-to,'" said Eddie with a laugh.

"Now you expect me to follow you out of here?" asked Commander Lytes, a taunting grin on his face.

"That's right," said Eddie. "Your people will be returning soon and I want them to see you formally surrender to us, not just hear it over the radio."

Commander Lytes' hand was still holding tight to the radio, but Eddie didn't care. The message had already been communicated, and he could tell from the red light that it wasn't broadcasting anymore. The commander was just holding onto anything he could, since it was all slipping away. People did the strangest things when they were about to be defeated.

"Remember before when you said that all I had left was my dignity?" asked Lytes.

"I believe I do," said Eddie, eying the Kezzin in front of him.

"Well, you were right. Soldiers like you and me have only our dignity." Commander Lytes lifted his chin with a new glint in eyes. "And we are truly nothing, and I mean *nothing*, without it!"

Eddie watched as Lytes' hands shot for something underneath the console, and he sprang forward when he saw the detonation box. It was clear, and inside was a large red button.

A failsafe, thought Eddie, halting and then jumping backward. He aimed the tri-rifle at the commander, but the gun shook in his hands as he kept falling backward to distance himself from whatever would explode from the console—a last-ditch suicidal effort to take everything out, mainframe included.

The commander pulled open the clear box and slammed his hand down on the button seconds before Eddie could steady the tri-rifle to fire.

But it was too late.

Too late to think, to stop the blast, to take cover, to breathe.

The explosion engulfed the room and took everything with it.

Omega-line Q-Ship, Nexus, Tangki System

Julianna watched from the air as the ground forces froze almost as one. They turned, looking toward the base.

Had they been called back? she mused.

But then she didn't have to wonder any longer. The Brotherhood soldiers turned and marched back, although their retreat formation was not as neat as the advance had been.

Over the distant waters of the ocean, the Stingrays swerved upward before turning their noses down in unison and barreling toward the rampant waters.

"Black Eagles, retreat to the shoreline. We know what's coming next, so do not engage," ordered Julianna over the comm.

Her squadron of Black Eagles headed back in her direction, but before they'd made it to land the Stingrays halted in mid-dive and leveled out. They slowed their speed, still a good distance from the Black Eagles.

"Woohoo!" yelled Julianna. "They've surrendered! The Captain did it! *We've* done it."

The land of Sunex was now covered with people whose faces were turned to the sky, but Julianna realized it had never come to that. The Black Eagles had lured the threat away, Lars had been successful in the ruse, and now Eddie had made the commander of the Brotherhood surrender. They'd defeated them with a fraction of the forces.

She looked at the base before racing the Q-Ship in that direction. Soon Eddie would be escorting Commander Lytes out of the Command Center to board his ship.

She was almost there when it happened. An explosion of orange and white and red rocketed into the sky and sent a wave of heat over Julianna's ship, buffeting her backward. The blast hurled debris into the air, and it landed all over the base. Chaos ensued and the Brotherhood fled as the Black Eagles swooped in. Julianna's head was muddled with confusion, but she flew straight into the smoke and realized exactly what had blown up. It had been the Command Center, and it was currently engulfed in flames.

The *Unsurpassed*, Nexus, Tangki System

On the bridge of his ship, Felix Castile watched the footage over and over again. Commander Lytes had blown up his post, which meant only one thing—his position had been compromised and he had been forced to surrender. Commander Lytes was not a likable male, but he had been a person of his word. He'd promised Felix that he'd die rather than be taken prisoner, to die with his secrets rather than be forced to spill them during interrogation.

A booming laugh erupted from Felix's mouth. Yes, the Federation had stopped him from taking over the planet of Nexus. Yes, he'd lost the commander of the Brotherhood army, and the army itself. However, they'd all been played. It would have been too good for this all to go according to plan. Felix knew it wouldn't, so he'd secretly been working on something else—something that would actually be the death of the Federation.

The Brotherhood army had been large and easy to track, of course, and would have caught the eyes of the Federation. He even suspected that the crafty hackers the Federation somehow had access to would spot their invasion of Nexus. That had almost been the *point*. While Ghost Squadron was busy stopping the takeover of an innocent planet, Felix had been securing the one thing he needed to finish his plan.

He knew that what General Lance Reynolds enjoyed most was his power. He *flaunted* it, telling the less powerful what they could or couldn't do, where they could or couldn't go. General Reynolds was the reason Felix was on this ship in space rather than on Earth where he belonged, but that was all going to change once the last part of the puzzle was in place.

Felix narrowed his eyes at the burning Command Center on the screen. Forces were working to put out the fire, but Felix didn't care. He put his back to the image.

Not only was he in a better position to complete his mission now, he'd managed to take out the Captain of Ghost Squadron while doing it. General Lance Reynolds would be livid. He'd know that Felix was that much closer to finishing him. He could feel the terror building in the General, and it made him giddy. Soon he'd stand face to face with Reynolds and make him pay for his injustices.

Felix hadn't actually needed an army, and he didn't need the armory of weapons, although they would come in handy, for sure. All he needed was what he was currently in possession of: the whereabouts of the most despicable man he'd ever met, and the means to bring him down.

Felix ground his teeth, his jaw clicking. General Lance Reynolds' time would soon be at an end, and Felix's face would be the last thing the old man ever saw.

EPILOGUE

QBS *ArchAngel*, Nexus, Tangki System

The light was too bright.

Wait, it wasn't bright enough.

He could see nothing. Eddie tried to blink, but it didn't do much to clear his vision. *Blackness.* There was glowing blackness everywhere. How could that be? How could black glow? How could he both see and not see?

He pulled in a breath, but it didn't feel like a breath. It felt like a grenade had gone off in his chest as the pressure erupted. He tried to grab at his heart, but his arms were locked in place.

Was this death? It sure felt like purgatory.

I thought I was going to hell, he thought, and tried to laugh. The sensation was weird. It felt like he was laughing while teetering on the edge of a cliff, or like he was smiling at his own funeral. *What was happening?* The blackness still blanketed his vision.

Eddie's tongue felt swollen as he tried to open his

mouth, and a strange metallic scum which tasted like gunpowder and soot coated it. That was when he realized the soot was in his nose, as if he'd inhaled the ashes of a camp fire.

Fire! The memory charged back into his mind like a dozen wild horses. The explosion. Commander Lytes. The Command Center. *The bomb.*

He was dead, and this was hell. It was all over—just an eternity of glowing blackness.

A creaking sound made him realize that his ears worked, or at least his hearing. He couldn't tell which, not with the new and different sensations all over his body.

"Is he ready?" asked a voice, one he recognized. It felt like it had been a hundred years since he had heard that voice, and it also felt like yesterday.

"Yes, it appears so," someone else said.

"Then why does he still sleep?" asked the other familiar voice.

"Don't you remember? You had to wake up on your own. You had to break out of it, kind of like being reborn," said the other person.

"I don't remember that, but it's been a long time," she said, her voice cool and calm and almost amused.

Eddie longed to push away the glowing darkness and drink something that would wash away the metallic taste in his mouth. To move his body...which... WHICH... His body felt different, brand new. Better than new —enhanced.

His eyes sprang open at once, and the light was so blinding he clapped his hands over his eyes. He'd had no idea that all he had to do was open his eyes. He'd been trapped by his own eyelids.

His hands now covered his eyes, which felt too tender to ever take in light again.

"Well, lookee there. Our baby bird has hatched," said Julianna with a laugh.

"Each one is different. I never see the same rebirth from the Pod-doc," the man beside her said in an amused voice.

Eddie peeled his hands away, and the light became a bit easier to take with each passing second. "I-I-I..." he stuttered, trying to find his voice. "I'm alive?"

Julianna peered down at him with a broad smile on her face, and her eyes twinkling. His vision felt brand new too, as if he were seeing her for the first time. "Well, you almost *weren't* alive anymore, but now you are. It was touch and go there for a long time, but we brought you back."

Eddie tried to push up, but found the task a bit difficult. His body was new, and it felt different. Everything seemed to take more effort on his part. "I'm alive?" he repeated.

"Yes, you definitely are," said Julianna. She offered him a hand and a smile. "Welcome back, Captain. We did what we had to, so they made a few changes to you. Hope you don't mind. It was that or death, and I wagered you weren't ready to rest yet."

FINIS

AUTHOR NOTES - SARAH NOFFKE

DECEMBER 19, 2017

One, two, three! I declare an Author's Notes war (like thumb war lol)! MA always gets to write his notes last, after reviewing mine. Which means he gets the last quip, however, I'll just keep writing books and see who is laughing last. Wait...never mind. That's not how that works.

So let's discuss what's on everyone's mind. It's not the tension simmering between the Captain and the Commander in this series. It's not that amazing fight speech that Julianna gives. Man, that's going to stay with you for hours, am I right? Great job to whoever crafted that Shakespearean gold. And it's not even the fact that Eddie is now upgraded. It's that Ricky Bobby scene. Am I right?

Author insight: MA and I, sat down and hammered out that scene because it's one of the few things that connects this series to the main one. We discussed the parting of ways between RB and Jules (that's what I call her, because this two name business is just too much. I won't even call my Michael by his name. I just call him And, which is hella confusing. And I digress. Bringing RB back for a resolution was a really fun time to collaborate and tie things together between the series. I also loved the opportunity to show the layers in Jules. I'm all about character development. I'll ponder on how a character ties their shoes because I think it's important and then I gloss over fight scenes.

I remember sending the Ricky Bobby scene to And. He cut it down, like a paper factory preparing for next year's Christmas card production. Anyway, I cried. Stomped around. And then I remembered that we're co-writers. Emphasis on co. We discussed and found a good balance. It was a growing moment because the perfect version was something in between what I had and what he wrote. So that's how this works. We color on each other's work. And just when I think And made my picture of a Care Bear all messed up, I realized he's highlighted its features.

I swear I don't do drugs. This is just my mad ramblings when they let me talk unfiltered. And I haven't even started cursing yet.

For fuck sake! It's time to thank some awesome readers who wrote our book for us. We often ask for input on names, drink ideas, or ideas in general. I'd like to thank the clever Natale Roberts for suggesting we use Douglas Adams as a drink. Oh and the Singapore Sling was all Barbara Twrawick Hasebe's idea. The bar scene with the brick wall is because of Lisa Frett's genius. And speaking of a genius, Micky Cocker is my new naming guru. She named Knox Gunnerson, Axel, Sabien and Alleira and many more. Randy Barber gets all the credit for the nipposes ouzo (great story, dude!). Great call there. And many of the ideas we included were due to the great input given to us by Ron Gailey, Tim Adams, Alastar Wilson, Lisa Frett and Charles Wood.

Okay, I guess I've rambled on here for long enough. I know you need time to roll that Jule's speech around in her head and reflect on your own purpose because of those words.

It's your turn, And!

Drops mic and walks away.

AUTHOR NOTES - MICHAEL ANDERLE

WRITTEN DECEMBER 20, 2017

The Author walks on stage, watching the diminutive blond author walk off the stage in the other direction as he continues onstage, waving at the crowd. Stopping at the middle, he looks down and raises one eye-brow. Bending over, he picks up the mic Noffke dropped and turns it over, looking for a big dent.

There isn't one.

He looks up and surveys the audience, the barest hint of a smirk is playing on his lips as he starts talking.

"So, three authors go into a bar." He smiles as he raises his eyebrows, "I know!" He shakes his head. "I am just as shocked and appalled as you are right now," he continues, waiting for a few chuckles to die down. "Can you believe that not one of those sumbitches come out? Why you ask?" He smiles broadly and throws out a hand, "Because those fuckers are still in there drinking and having a good time!"

<Massive hooting and hollering ensues, because those in the audience *are people just like us.*>

And they get that is how we are as authors.

Well, those that I'm working with. I can't speak to the 'authordom' at large. I have watched different groups of people over my many years and I'm fairly sure that the creative bent that helps us be authors affects the greater proportion of authors to be *different*.

Sometimes, it affects us in ways that kinda suck, but kinda work. The massively introverted author who can't stand crowds, but is yearning with all their heart for a lifetime to just fit in with their own people.

For some, it causes emotional problems that we suffer with through our full life.

For others, they are the direct opposite.

For a few, we find our tribe, and our acceptance amongst our tribe. Whether it is two of us partying in San Diego for a work weekend (and hell yes, I would write that trip off on the jet boat. Because I would use that experience in my books) or a handful.

Or a hundred, or even fifteen thousand (20booksTo50k on Facebook).

I was blessed to read a fan comment on a Facebook post this afternoon that spoke to how they felt they had found a tribe in the LMBPN family of authors (Kurtherian and Oriceran groups specifically.) This post made my afternoon.

My co-authors, collaborators, and just plain friends are all over the world. We are united by loving to read stories, and some of us by writing them. Further, we love the fact that we, the Indie Outlaws, are able to do something cool for others.

And we fucking *do* it.

We continue to give away Kindles, connect to Vets, support troops, and engage with you because *we need it too.*

If we lose our energy, you are there to lend us some of yours. If we are reaching for the finish line, you encourage us to write and to cross it. When we think our latest story is inadequate, you give us the feedback we need.

I said all of that to say *Thank You* for a fantastic 2017!

I could not have done what I did with these collaborators, without you supporting us and giving these stories a chance.

Ad Aeternitatem,
Michael

ACKNOWLEDGMENTS

SARAH NOFFKE

Thank you to Michael Anderle for taking my calls and allowing me to play in this universe. It's been a blast since the beginning.

Thank you to Craig Martelle for cheering for me. I've learned so much working with you. This wild ride just keeps going and going.

Thank you to Jen, Tim, Steve, Andrew and Jeff for all the work on the books, covers and championing so much of the publishing.

Thank you to our beta team. I can't believe how fast you all can turn around books. The JIT team sometimes scares me, but usually just with how impressively knowledgeable they are.

Thank you to our amazing readers. I asked myself a question the other day and it had a strange answer. I asked if I would still write if trapped on a desert island and no one would ever read the books. The answer was yes, but the feeling connected to it was different. It wouldn't be as much fun to write if there wasn't awesome readers to share it with. Thank you.

Thank you to my friends and family for all the support and love.

SNEAK PEEK OF DEGENERATION

Turn the page for an excerpt from
Degeneration
(The Ghost Squadron, Book #4)

CHAPTER 1

Planet Sagano, Behemoth System

Heat blasted Eddie in the face as he ducked under some fallen trees, and he stayed in a crouch as he sprinted through the burning jungle. The fire at his back was growing in intensity, although the crews had been fighting it for days.

A loud *crack* overhead tore his attention in that direction. The fire had overwhelmed a large stand of trees, which fell in on each other until the largest chose the direction they were going to fall. Eddie rolled to the side, dirt and ash raining down on him as the burning trees hit the ground exactly where he'd been.

He didn't pause, but rather dashed forward to clear the next part of the burning forest. His vision blurred from his incredible speed, and his feet hardly felt as though they touched the soft ground before rising again.

Flames licked the side of a building, having jumped from some nearby branches, but Eddie sped up the ladder to the house, which had been built on stilts. Entering a burning building was one thing, but entering one that was held up by wooden poles in the middle of a forest fire was something else entirely. None of this seemed at all like a good idea.

Too bad he didn't have a choice.

The trap door at the top opened and then slammed over as Eddie spilled into the jungle hut. He scanned the room, and the smoke burned his eyes. The living space was open but there were some rooms at the back, so he ran in that direction while wiping tears out of his eyes.

He kicked the first door open and searched the room, which was empty. The structure rocked, probably from the fire consuming the front of the house, which was where the next set of rooms was located.

Without hesitating, Eddie darted for the next room and rammed his shoulder into the door, ripping it off its hinges. He still wasn't used to his enhanced strength. After all, he'd only had this body for a short time.

Eddie pivoted to the adjacent wall and shot his foot straight at the door. The following area was empty at first glance and fire licked through the open window, spilling smoke into the space. Eddie covered his face from the blaze and was just about to turn back when something caught his eyes.

On the far side of the room between the wall and the bed was a small boy.

Thank the fucking stars! Eddie thought, relief swelling in his chest. "Come on!" yelled Eddie, extending a hand to the kid, who was about four years old. The boy's large eyes stared at the intruding fire, and his face was swollen and red from the heat.

"It's okay! Come on, pal," said Eddie. He dashed forward and scooped the kid into his arms, the heat more intense on that side of the room. "Hold on to me."

The child clutched Eddie's neck tightly and his legs wrapped around his waist.

Eddie ducked as much as he could with the boy attached to him, and ran out. Eddie could hear the boy sobbing, although it was barely audible over the sound of the fire destroying the house. He wrapped an arm around the child's back and shielded his eyes from the smoke, which was thicker now, with the other.

"It's going to be all right," said Eddie, screaming to be heard over the crackling flames.

The boy vibrated with terror as Eddie carried him back to the trap door and ladder. The house rocked again, this time sliding forward, and Eddie lost his footing and slipped. The floor was at an angle now, and the stilts weren't going to stay upright much longer. Eddie realized that they were at the bottom of the house, so if it fell over they'd be crushed in the burning destruction.

Eddie threw his weight and that of the small child forward to try to make up the ground they'd lost when the building tilted. He pressed his boots hard into the tilted floor, but it felt as though he were trying to climb a slick mountain.

The fire had now overtaken most of the main living area, and it was closing in on them fast. Without a second glance Eddie shuffled over to the ladder and clumsily crouched, locating the first rung with his boot. It was harder to manage with the boy clenched to his front, but there was no time to change positions.

"Hold on tight," he said to the boy. "We're getting out of here!"

The child nodded against Eddie's chest, his face pushing into him hard. Eddie climbed down, although now the ladder was leaning. The fire had crawled under the house and was eating at two of the four stilts and, now overhead, the wooden floor creaked and ached.

A loud *crack* shook the structure and the house dropped two feet. The boy's body tensed against Eddie's torso as his gaze flew to the stilt on the right, which had splintered and was barely holding.

The house groaned, fire now spreading over the floor above them and heading for the ladder.

Making an impromptu decision, Eddie jumped backward off the ladder, wrapping his arms around the child as they plummeted down. By crouching as they hit he relieved the brunt of the fall, and now, finally on the ground, he hunched over and started running.

A tumultuous *crash* echoed behind them. The house was leaning aggressively forward and it started to fall, so Eddie kicked it into high gear and barreled away faster than he had ever run ever before. The heat from the fire seared his back, and smoke and fire shot from the building as it crashed to the ground right behind him. He'd barely made it out! He kept running as trees toppled toward him in the wake of the collapse of the burning house.

The rush of heat made Eddie's skin feel like it was melting, but he kept his head tucked and pressed the boy against him as he sped back the way he'd come. *Only a little farther,* he said to himself, unable to say anything aloud. He wasn't out of breath from running, but rather from the smoke he'd been inhaling since this started.

Fire had taken over most of the jungle, and it was closing in on them. Eddie leapt over a burning log since he didn't see a clear path around it, then ducked under a curtain of vines and leaves, smoking and singed at the ends. Soon the entire area would be engulfed.

The boy jostled Eddie's body oddly, but his weight didn't slow him down. The threat of burning to death was motivation enough for him to hurtle through the flames, but finally Eddie burst into a clearing where the ground was already charred and the tree stumps still smoking. The fire had already consumed the trees and since been extinguished. This had been where it all started.

Eddie halted, and after heaving in a giant breath he tried to unclasp the boy's hands from behind his neck. For a little guy he was strong, and clearly not willing to let go.

"Hey, buddy. You're okay. You're safe," said Eddie, patting the kid on the back gently. The child relaxed a little and slowly pulled away, staring at him with large brown eyes. He cried softly, tears glistening down his cheeks.

"That's it. Take a breath. It's okay," said Eddie.

"Dracott!" a woman yelled in the distance. She ran in their direction with her brown hair flying behind her.

The boy whipped his head around, and another sob emerged from his mouth. He pushed away from Eddie eagerly now, dropping to his feet and sprinting for the woman. "Mommy!" yelled Dracott.

When the two met on the charred ground, the woman grabbed her son and cradled him to her. She was shaking and crying as she clutched the boy, pinning him into her chest.

Eddie strode toward them, seeking refuge from the heat of the fire at his back. In the distance he saw the team, who were tirelessly trying to quell the stubborn fire which had taken over this part of the jungle and was destroying many homes and much animal habitat.

When Eddie approached, Dracott's arms were wrapped around his mother's neck and his head resting on her shoulder like he was ready for a nap after the whole ordeal. The woman rubbed her son's lean back, tears still puddling in her eyes.

"Thank you, sir. I cannot thank you enough for what you did," said the woman, her voice vibrating with relief.

Eddie smiled at the mother and son, finally reunited.

Julianna approached from the side. She had a sly smile on her face, and didn't seem relieved to see him safe after entering the forest fire.

"You're absolutely welcome," said Eddie to the woman. "Now, you two should get as far from the fire as possible. Dracott has inhaled a lot of smoke."

The woman nodded and carried her son away.

"You weren't worried about me, were you?" Eddie asked Julianna when she paused beside him to stare at the retreating woman and child.

"When did I have time to worry? I was timing you," joked Julianna.

A laugh popped from his mouth. "What was my time?"

"Two minutes and ten seconds," answered Julianna.

"And you didn't worry even a little bit?" asked Eddie.

Julianna cut her eyes at him. "Maybe toward the end,

but I knew you were going to drag that boy to safety one way or another."

"Poor kid! He was terrified," said Eddie.

"Yeah, fires like this bring chaos. It was a shame that he got lost, but at least you jumped in to save him," said Julianna.

Eddie surveyed the burning jungle. "What do you think? Is there more we can do here?"

"The fire crew says they could use an extra few hands on the eastern perimeter. They're trying to fence in the fires there," said Julianna.

Eddie slapped his hands together, rubbing them eagerly. They'd had Pip monitor the radios, listening for disasters on nearby planets just so Eddie could swoop in and do something brave. That was how he was breaking in his newly enhanced body.

"I'm ready! Let's do this," said Eddie, ambling forward.

"You think you're going to get this adventuring out of your system soon?" asked Julianna from beside him.

"Does it ever wear off, having these enhancements?" he asked.

"No, not really. Not for me, anyway," said Julianna.

Eddie grinned. "Then no. What's the point in having this body and not using it?"

THE GHOST SQUADRON

by Sarah Noffke and Michael Anderle

WANT MORE?

ENTER

THE KURTHERIAN GAMBIT UNIVERSE

A desperate move by a dying alien race transforms the unknown world into an ever-expanding, paranormal, intergalactic force.

The Kurtherian Gambit Universe contains more than 100 titles in series created by Michael Anderle and many talented co-authors. For a complete list of books in this phenomenal marriage of paranormal and science fiction, go to:

http://kurtherianbooks.com/timeline-kurtherian/

ABOUT SARAH NOFFKE

Sarah Noffke, an Amazon Best Seller, writes YA and NA sci-fi fantasy, paranormal and urban fantasy. She is the author of the Lucidites, Reverians, Ren, Vagabond Circus, Olento Research and Soul Stone Mage series. Noffke holds a Masters of Management and teaches college business courses. Most of her students have no idea that she toils away her hours crafting fictional characters. Noffke's books are top rated and best-sellers on Kindle. Currently, she has eighteen novels published. Her books are available in paperback, audio and in Spanish, Portuguese and Italian.

SARAH NOFFKE SOCIAL

Website: http://www.sarahnoffke.com
Facebook: https://www.facebook.com/officialsarahnoffke
Amazon: http://amzn.to/1JGQjRn

THE SOUL STONE MAGE SERIES

House of Enchanted #1

The Kingdom of Virgo has lived in peace for thousands of years...until now.

The humans from Terran have always been real assholes to the witches of Virgo. Now a silent war is brewing, and the timing couldn't be worse. Princess Azure will soon be crowned queen of the Kingdom of Virgo.

In the Dark Forest a powerful potion-maker has been murdered.

Charmsgood was the only wizard who could stop a deadly virus plaguing Virgo. He also knew about the devastation the people from Terran had done to the forest.

Azure must protect her people. Mend the Dark Forest. Create alliances with savage beasts. No biggie, right?

But on coronation day everything changes. Princess Azure isn't who she thought she was and that's a big freaking problem.

Welcome to The Revelations of Oriceran.

The Dark Forest #2

Mountain of Truth #3

Land of Terran #4

New Egypt #5

Lancothy #6

Awoken, #1:

Around the world humans are hallucinating after sleepless nights. In a sterile, underground institute the forecasters keep reporting the same events. And in the backwoods of Texas, a sixteen-year-old girl is about to be caught up in a fierce, ethereal battle.

Meet Roya Stark. She drowns every night in her dreams, spends her hours reading classic literature to avoid her family's ridicule, and is prone to premonitions—which are becoming more frequent. And now her dreams are filled with strangers offering to reveal what she has always wanted to know: Who is she? That's the question that haunts her, and she's about to find out. But will Roya live to regret learning the truth?

Stunned, #2

Revived, #3

Defects, #1

In the happy, clean community of Austin Valley, everything appears to be perfect. Seventeen-year-old Em Fuller, however, fears something is askew. Em is one of the new generation of Dream Travelers. For some reason, the gods have not seen fit to gift all of them with their expected special abilities. Em is a Defect—one of the unfortunate Dream Travelers not gifted with a psychic power. Desperate to do whatever it takes to earn her gift, she endures painful daily injections along with commands from her overbearing, loveless father. One of the few bright spots in her life is the return of a friend she had thought dead—but with his return comes the knowledge of a shocking, unforgivable truth. The society Em thought was protecting her has actually been betraying her, but she has no idea how to break away from its authority without hurting everyone she loves.

Rebels, #2

Warriors, #3

VAGABOND CIRCUS SERIES

Suspended, #1

When a stranger joins the cast of Vagabond Circus—a circus that is run by Dream Travelers and features real magic—mysterious events start happening. The once orderly grounds of the circus become riddled with hidden threats. And the ringmaster realizes not only are his circus and its magic at risk, but also his very life.

Vagabond Circus caters to the skeptics. Without skeptics, it would close its doors. This is because Vagabond Circus runs for two reasons and only two reasons: first and foremost to provide the lost and lonely Dream Travelers a place to be illustrious. And secondly, to show the nonbelievers that there's still magic in the world. If they believe, then they care, and if they care, then they don't destroy. They stop the small abuse that day-by-day breaks down humanity's spirit. If Vagabond Circus makes one skeptic believe in magic, then they halt the cycle, just a little bit. They allow a little more love into this world. That's Dr. Dave Raydon's mission. And that's why this ringmaster recruits. That's why he directs. That's why he puts on a show that makes people question their beliefs. He wants the world to believe in magic once again.

Paralyzed, #2

Released, #3

Ren: The Man Behind the Monster, #1

Born with the power to control minds, hypnotize others, and read thoughts, Ren Lewis, is certain of one thing: God made a mistake. No one should be born with so much power. A monster awoke in him the same year he received his gifts. At ten years old. A prepubescent boy with the ability to control others might merely abuse his powers, but Ren allowed it to corrupt him. And since he can have and do anything he wants, Ren should be happy. However, his journey teaches him that harboring so much power doesn't bring happiness, it steals it. Once this realization sets in, Ren makes up his mind to do the one thing that can bring his tortured soul some peace. He must kill the monster.

Note This book is NA and has strong language, violence and sexual references.

Ren: God's Little Monster, #2

Ren: The Monster Inside the Monster, #3

Ren: The Monster's Adventure, #3.5

Ren: The Monster's Death, #4

OLENTO RESEARCH SERIES

Alpha Wolf, #1:

Twelve men went missing.

Six months later they awake from drug-induced stupors to find themselves locked in a lab.

And on the night of a new moon, eleven of those men, possessed by new—and inhuman—powers, break out of their prison and race through the streets of Los Angeles until they disappear one by one into the night.

Olento Research wants its experiments back. Its CEO, Mika Lenna, will tear every city apart until he has his werewolves imprisoned once again. He didn't undertake a huge risk just to lose his would-be assassins.

However, the Lucidite Institute's main mission is to save the world from injustices. Now, it's Adelaide's job to find these mutated men and protect them and society, and fast. Already around the nation, wolflike men are being spotted. Attacks on innocent women are happening. And then, Adelaide realizes what her next step must be: She has to find the alpha wolf first. Only once she's located him can she stop whoever is behind this experiment to create wild beasts out of human beings.

Lone Wolf, #2

Rabid Wolf, #3

Bad Wolf, #4

Printed in Great Britain
by Amazon